His kiss was raw and primal.

Inside Jess, fear and desire clashed, like steel dragged across rock at a high rate of speed, shooting sparks high into the air.

It was crazy, considering what they were about to do, but she kissed Madrid back. Turning her back to the danger that lurked outside, she allowed herself to revel in the feel of his mouth against hers, his hands on her body. "What was that for?" she asked when he pulled back.

"Luck."

"If that was for luck," she said breathlessly, "I'm afraid to imagine what'll happen when we finish this."

Taking her hand, Madrid stepped out into the darkness of midnight, ready to face the devil in his den. She followed, her mind numb to the danger. Instead, her mind was reeling, her body vibrating with the aftershocks of his kiss. It was silly to think about an inconsequential kiss when they were about to risk their lives. But there was nothing inconsequential about the way Madrid had kissed her.

There *would* be consequences...

LINDA CASTILLO

OPERATION: MIDNIGHT RENDEZVOUS

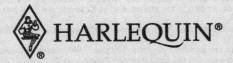

HARLEQUIN®

TORONTO • NEW YORK • LONDON
AMSTERDAM • PARIS • SYDNEY • HAMBURG
STOCKHOLM • ATHENS • TOKYO • MILAN • MADRID
PRAGUE • WARSAW • BUDAPEST • AUCKLAND

ISBN-13: 978-0-373-88714-9
ISBN-10:   0-373-88714-0

OPERATION: MIDNIGHT RENDEZVOUS

Copyright: © 2006 by Linda Castillo

ABOUT THE AUTHOR

Linda Castillo knew at a very young age that she wanted to be a writer—and penned her first novel at the age of thirteen. She is the winner of numerous writing awards, including the Holt Medallion, the Golden Heart and the Daphne du Maurier and she received a nomination for the prestigious RITA® Award.

Linda loves writing edgy romantic suspense novels that push the envelope and take her readers on a roller-coaster ride of breathtaking romance and thrilling suspense. She resides in Texas with her husband, four lovable dogs and an Appaloosa named George. For a complete list of her books, check out her Web site at www.lindacastillo.com. Contact her at books@lindacastillo.com. Or write to her at P.O. Box 670501, Dallas, Texas 75367-0501.

Books by Linda Castillo

HARLEQUIN INTRIGUE
871—OPERATION: MIDNIGHT TANGO
890—OPERATION: MIDNIGHT ESCAPE
920—OPERATION: MIDNIGHT GUARDIAN
940—OPERATION: MIDNIGHT RENDEZVOUS

CAST OF CHARACTERS

Jessica Atwood—Accused of a murder she didn't commit, she fled the police with her best friend's little boy in tow. But the police weren't the only ones looking for her—or the child. Can she find out who framed her and clear her name before the real killers finish the job they began?

Mike Madrid—The MIDNIGHT agent was Angela's former partner—and lover. Determined to find her killer, he lays down his badge and vows to find the killer and bring them to justice. But he soon finds himself falling for his number one suspect.

Angela Matheson—The MIDNIGHT agent and young mother was murdered while working deep undercover as a dirty cop in the small, coastal town of Lighthouse Point, California. Did she get too close to discovering the idyllic town's dark secret?

Nicholas Matheson—A special-needs child witnessed his mother's murder. Unable to speak, he must now rely on his mom's best friend to keep him safe from the bad man.

Sean Cutter—Head of the MIDNIGHT Agency, he deemed Mike Madrid too emotionally involved to work the case. But when Madrid turns in his badge and goes rogue, Cutter has no recourse but to let him go.

Norm Mummert—The chief of police of Lighthouse Point, California, he is a by-the-book cop determined to find the person responsible for the death of one of his officers. Or is he?

Jake Vanderpol—The MIDNIGHT agent and personal friend Mike Madrid called upon as a last resort. Will Jake risk his career and reputation to help his fellow agent?

Prologue

Jessica Atwood ran blindly through the darkness. Around her, rain poured down in icy sheets. Trees and brush slashed at her face and clothes; mud sucked at her shoes like quicksand. She plowed through the branches and fought her way through the heavy brush, her labored breaths rushing between clenched teeth. Her lungs burned as if they were on fire, but she didn't stop.

She would die before she let them hurt the boy.

Gripping his hand tighter, she ran. Behind her she could hear them shouting. Razor blades of light cut through the night as the powerful beams of their flashlights sought her. In the distance she could hear the dogs baying. Gaining ground. Death knocking on her door.

"Come on, baby," she panted. "Run for me. Run!"

When Nicolas didn't respond, she squeezed his hand. Vaguely she was aware of him crying. She wanted to hold him, tell him everything was going to be all right. But there wasn't time. They were running for their lives.

Terror was like a wild beast turned loose inside her. She knew their pursuers would kill them both if they caught them. She couldn't let that happen. Couldn't let them kill an innocent child. Somehow she had to save them.

Or die trying.

The first gunshot exploded like a bomb. A scream tore from her throat when a branch fractured less than a foot from her head. Shoving Nicolas ahead to keep him out of the line of fire, she darted left and took him down a ravine at a reckless speed.

"Run!" she panted. "Please, baby. Faster!"

They hit the foot of the gully in an all-out sprint. She glanced back to see one of their pursuers at the top of the ravine, silhouetted against the night sky. Terror ratcheted into something wild and unwieldy when she saw him raise his rifle for a shot.

Oh, dear God, no! she thought, and picked up speed. An instant later something struck her left arm with what seemed to be the force of a missile traveling at the speed of light. The impact spun her around, and the violent shock of pain sent her to her knees. A second later the report shattered the night.

"Mah-mah. Mah-mah!"

She glanced at Nicolas, at the tears and mud that streaked his face. He needed her. She had to be strong. She had to get them through this. Angela would have wanted that for her son.

"I'm okay, honey," she said.

"Mah-mah." He reached for her, his face crumpling. "Mah-mah!"

"It's going to be all right." Cradling her injured arm, she staggered to her feet. Pain clutched her like a giant, bony hand, and dizziness descended, but she shook it off and grabbed Nicolas's hand.

"Come on," she whispered.

Animal sounds tore from her throat as she stumbled over rocks and tree roots and loose dirt. She lost her footing twice, but somehow managed to stay upright. At a dangerous speed they descended into a second ravine. Midway down, Jess's foot caught on something and she fell, screaming when Nicolas's hand was torn from hers. She went into a wild tumble, rocks and tree roots battering her body, but all she could think about was Nicolas, alone and in danger.

The earth disappeared beneath her then, catapulting her into a free fall. Jess knew that when she landed the impact would surely kill her. Instead, her body slammed into water. The sudden sharp cold shocked her system and she went under. As the strong current pulled her downstream, debris hit her and the churning water tumbled her. Stifling a scream, she sucked in a mouthful of water and began to choke. Panic gripped her. Fighting it, she kicked her legs hard and fast and an instant later her face broke the surface.

"Nicolas!" she screamed.

She struggled against the powerful current, but the force of the water swept her along the jagged bank dotted with rocks and tree roots. She tried to look around, but all she saw was darkness and rain and black, swirling water.

"Nicolas!"

But when she reached for his hand all she felt was the cold grip of the river. All she heard was the whisper of death in her ear.

Chapter One

Mike Madrid knew something big was going down the instant the call came in on his secure line at four o'clock in the morning. The call itself wasn't unusual, considering he worked for a top secret agency. He knew it was bad when Sean Cutter refused to give him details over the phone.

"I want you at MIDNIGHT headquarters by oh five hundred," Cutter said.

Madrid made the drive from his apartment in an upscale Washington, D.C., neighborhood to the top secret MIDNIGHT Agency headquarters in record time. He'd expected Cutter to have already assembled the team for whatever assignment had warranted the call out, but he found only one man in the room. When Sean Cutter looked up from where he sat, Madrid suddenly knew this wasn't about an assignment or a mission. It was personal.

"What happened?" he asked without preamble.

"Sit down."

"I don't want to sit down." Madrid's heart began to pound. "I want to know what the hell is going on."

Cutter leaned back in his chair. Within the depths of his eyes Madrid saw knowledge. He saw regret. Caution. Worst of all he saw a damnable amount of sympathy. "We lost an agent last night."

"Who?" But even before Cutter answered, he knew.

"Angela Matheson."

The name struck him like a brass-knuckle punch. Disbelief and grief tangled inside him, but Madrid didn't let himself react. A master at schooling his expression and body language, he stood perfectly still, his face carefully blank, his eyes level on his superior.

"You sure?" he asked after a moment, surprised his voice sounded so normal when he was coming apart inside.

"Yeah."

"How did it happen?"

"She was on assignment in Northern California. Deep undercover work."

"Are you being vague on purpose?"

"You know how it works."

A deep-cover operative himself, Madrid knew all too well that the fewer people who knew about an operation, the better the chance that the agent's cover would remain intact. He shouldn't take Cutter's silence personally, but he did.

"Did someone make her?" he asked. "Blow her cover? What?"

"We don't know the details."

"I'm not in the mood to be stonewalled."

"Then stop asking questions I can't answer." Cutter sighed tiredly, and Madrid realized the other man had been up all night. "Look, I didn't want you to hear about this secondhand. That's why I called you in."

Madrid didn't want this to be about emotions. It was about the loss of an agent. But he could feel the emotions burgeoning inside him. "You put someone on it?"

"I did."

"Who?"

Cutter frowned.

Madrid smiled, but the stretching of his lips belied the emotions slashing his insides to bits. "You know better than to try to lock me out of this."

"I know better than to assign an agent something when he's too personally involved."

"I'm not some damn rookie, Sean. I can handle it."

"No dice, Mike."

Fury joined the chorus of emotions singing through him. "What about the boy?" Nicolas, he remembered. A sweet kid with special needs.

"Missing."

The word hit him like a punch. Angela had loved that kid more than anything in the world. He wiped his wet palms on his slacks. "Why would someone take her kid? Was it a kidnapping? What?"

"We don't know yet."

Liar. "Do you have a suspect?"

Cutter's jaw flexed. The silence that followed spoke more than a thousand words.

"Witnesses? Anything at all to go on?"

"We think the boy witnessed her murder."

The knot in Madrid's chest tightened. Poor kid. "Aw, man."

"I'm sorry," Cutter said after a moment.

The last thing Madrid wanted was sympathy. "If you want to make me feel better, give me this assignment."

Cutter grimaced, softened. "Mike, I know you and Angela were...close."

"It was a long time ago. She was a friend. That's all."

Judging from the look on his face, the other man wasn't buying it.

Madrid didn't waste his time asking any more questions. Cutter wasn't going to tell him what he needed to know, and time was of the essence if he was going to bring that boy home. There were multitudes of ways to glean information, a task Madrid had always been very good at.

Reaching into his jacket, he removed his MID-NIGHT identification badge from his wallet. Next he tugged the Beretta .380 from his shoulder holster and set both on the conference-room table.

Cutter shook his head. "Don't do this, Mike."

"Then give me this case. Tell me what I need to know."

"You know I can't do that. Damn it, this isn't about revenge."

Another smile twisted Madrid's mouth. "It's always about revenge," he said, and walked out the door without looking back.

MIKE MADRID WAS LIKE a bloodhound when it came to tracking killers. Once he had the scent, there was no stopping him. After speaking with Cutter, he went back to his place and began calling in favors. He put his not-so-aboveboard computer skills to work and hacked a secure database the feds had deemed unhackable. Within hours he had a name.

Jessica Atwood.

Twenty-eight years old. Waitress. Recent messy divorce. From Phoenix. No children. No immediate family. She and Angela had gone to college together some ten years ago. Atwood didn't have a record, but Madrid knew that didn't mean she wasn't capable of murder. Under the right circumstances everyone was capable of murder. The burning question now was what did she want with the kid?

He caught a flight from D.C. to Sacramento and drove straight to the small town of Lighthouse Point on the coast. Located on Luna Bay, the town was a shipping port and as picturesque as a turn-of-the-century seascape.

Surprisingly, no other MIDNIGHT agent's were in sight. Some could be there, undercover, he knew but in his mind, the MIDNIGHT Agency should have been all over this. After all, one of their own had been taken out by a killer.

"I can't believe Angela is gone," chief of police Norm Mummert said with a shake of his head.

The chief's office had been his first stop. Madrid had identified himself as an investigator with the U.S. attorney's office out of San Francisco. Thanks to his vast stock of fake IDs, he had the credentials to back it up. But no one had questioned him.

"Angela was a police officer?" he asked.

"One of my best."

"Tell me about Atwood," Madrid said.

"She seemed nice enough. Pretty and young. She was staying with Angela. From what I understand they went to college together."

"They were friends?"

Mummert nodded. "I made some calls and found out Atwood had some trouble back home."

"What kind of trouble?"

"Divorce. Things got ugly. She took some money and ran. She needed a place to stay. Angela opened her door." He shook his head so hard his jowls shook. "I never had Atwood pegged as a killer."

"Do you have evidence that she is?"

The chief looked at him as if he were dense. "She attacked my officer with a knife and made off with the boy. Her prints were all over the place, including the murder weapon."

"Motive?"

"Hard to tell. We suspect she was after the child. It's the only scenario that could even begin to explain this terrible tragedy."

Mummert was a rotund man with sagging eyes and a drooping lower lip. Even though Angela had been murdered less than twenty-four hours ago, he looked as if he'd been up for a week. "Angela was like a daughter to me. She was a good police officer and a friend."

"Any idea where Atwood is headed?" Madrid asked.

The chief sighed. "I've got every available officer working on this. The state police have put out an APB. I swear it's like she disappeared off the face of the earth."

"Maybe she had an accomplice who picked her up."

"We were pretty quick setting up roadblocks. I don't think that's the case."

Having gleaned all the information he was going to get here, Madrid rose and extended his hand. "Thanks for your time. I'll be in touch."

On the sidewalk in front of the police station, Madrid looked around the small town of Lighthouse Point and wondered what Angela had been doing here. She'd been posing as a police officer. He wondered if her assignment had gotten her killed. The old emotions taunted him with unexpected force—emotions he would be a fool to acknowledge when he had a killer to find.

He got into the rental car and started the engine. He'd already been to the crime scene, seen the bloodstains and the trashed house. Though he'd processed dozens of crime scenes over the years, this one had shaken him badly.

Putting his hands on the steering wheel, he looked around the small town. "Where did you run?" he whispered.

He knew where Atwood had last been seen. The area had been thoroughly searched by cops on foot and in a helicopter equipped with infrared. Scent dogs had been deployed. The police were baffled that she'd escaped.

But Madrid had a distinct advantage over other law enforcement officials. An advantage not even his fellow MIDNIGHT agents possessed. He'd known Angela Matheson on a personal level. He knew her hopes. Her dreams.

He knew her secrets.

He knew Angela kept an undisclosed refuge.

Most undercover operatives did, on the outside chance they needed to lie low during a mission.

From what I understand they went to college together.

The police chief's words reverberated in his head. Words that reiterated the fact that Jessica Atwood and Angela had once been friends. There was a distinct possibility Angela had told Jessica Atwood about the cottage, particularly if Atwood was on the run from some abusive husband. Located on Wind River Island just a mile off the jagged coastline, it would make the perfect hideaway.

Finding her there might be a long shot, but Madrid had always been a gambler. He knew from experience that sometimes a long shot paid off.

"You can run," he said aloud as he pulled away from the curb. "But you can't hide."

THE WATER SURROUNDING Wind River Island was fraught with dangerous undercurrents and high surf; not many people ventured to the small, heavily forested island. There were two marinas in Lighthouse Point, and within the hour Madrid was able to ascertain that Angela had owned an open fisherman named *Riptide*.

Though she hadn't signed it out, the boat was not in its slip.

He waited until dusk and rented a decent-size fishing boat under the pretense of partaking in some early season king salmon fishing. But instead of going upriver where the salmon were beginning to spawn, he headed out to sea.

With a storm barreling in from the northwest, the heavy surf tossed the boat as if it were a toy. It took every nautical skill Madrid possessed to maneuver the treacherous waters. Using the lighthouse on the south side of the island as a beacon, he finally located the only inlet. It was nearly midnight when he docked at a dilapidated pier and tied off. By the light of a three-quarter moon he set out on foot to find Angela's killer.

The island was small, but on foot and operating in darkness, he took an hour to find the cottage. It was a rustic clapboard structure nestled in a sparse forest of hemlock and cedar. The cottage was built on a precipitous slope. On the west side, high cliffs ran a hundred feet down to where an angry sea battered the rocky shore.

The perfect place for a safe house.

Pulling his .40-caliber rubber-grip Taurus from his shoulder holster, Madrid approached the cottage from the rear. There was no smoke coming from the chimney. If Atwood was there, she was being careful. But he could see a dim light coming from inside.

"Gotcha," he whispered, anticipation whipping through him.

He slithered along the siding at the rear of the cottage and peered around the corner. A screened porch overlooked a tangle of wind-mangled hemlock. He could hear the roar of the surf below. Holding the pistol ready, he stepped around the corner.

"Don't give me a reason to kill you."

He jerked at the sound of the female voice coming from directly behind him. For an instant he considered spinning, firing and maybe getting off a lucky shot. But the sound of a bullet being chambered changed his mind.

"Drop the gun," she said. "Now."

Madrid couldn't believe he'd let a woman get the drop on him. A *civilian*. Not only was it humiliating, but dangerous. His ego was just big enough to be more bothered by the former than the latter.

"You got me," he said, and dropped the Taurus.

"Get your hands up."

He did as he was told.

"Turn around. Slowly."

More disgusted with himself than frightened, he turned. The sight of her shocked him, like electricity snapping through every nerve ending in his body. She was not what he'd expected. Though he'd seen photos of her in the course of his research, none of them did justice to the doe-eyed beauty holding that deadly looking pistol.

"Who are you and what do you want?" she demanded.

"My name is Mike Madrid," he said easily. "I'm a federal agent, and I'm looking for you."

She blinked as if she hadn't been expecting him to admit the truth so readily. Madrid studied her. Even in the dim light slanting through the window, he could see that she was small, but athletically built. She wore snug jeans and an oversize sweatshirt that revealed little of her figure beneath. But Madrid had a good imagination, especially when it came to women. He figured she was curvy in all the right places. A hell of a thought for him to be having when he was pretty sure this was going to end badly.

Her hair looked somewhere between blond and brown and fell in unruly tendrils to her slender shoulders. Her eyes were the same gray-blue as the ocean pounding the beach below. Her bow-shaped mouth was full and, despite the worried frown, perfect for kissing.

Not that he was going to be kissing her, he reminded himself. He might have a weakness for beautiful, dangerous women, but he drew the line at fraternizing with a cop killer.

"Why are you looking for me?" she asked.

"Because I'm going to take you in."

She laughed, but it was a hopeless, humorless sound. "Get inside. Now." She jabbed the gun toward the house.

"Whatever you say."

That was when he noticed the sheen of perspiration on her forehead. Her complexion was ghastly pale, but her cheeks were tinged pink. Her eyes had a glassiness to them he hadn't noticed before. A glassiness that wasn't caused by adrenaline or fear. Drugs? he wondered, and prayed she hadn't hurt the boy.

"Where's the kid?" he asked as he opened the door.

"I don't know what you're talking about."

He stepped inside and turned to her, careful to keep his hands up. "Give him to me and I'll let you walk away from this."

Anger flickered in her eyes. But the gun

wavered as she closed the door behind her. "Why are you so interested in the kid?"

"Because I don't want him hurt."

"Or maybe you want to finish what you started." Her teeth pulled back in a snarl that was distinctly feline, and she jammed the gun at him. "Here's a news flash for you. I will not let you hurt that child. You got that, slick?"

Madrid was adept at reading people. Now his well-honed instincts were telling him this woman truly believed he meant the child harm. But why would she think that when she was the one who'd kidnapped him and murdered his mother? Was she mentally unbalanced? Psychologically unstable? Or was there something else going on he didn't know about?

"The police found Angela's body," he said. "You're the prime suspect. Surely you know you're not going to get away with this."

"I did not kill Angela." Her voice broke on the name, but she took a shaky breath and continued. "She was my friend. She was helping me."

"Your prints are on the murder weapon."

"I picked it up, but I didn't use it."

"You took the boy."

"To save his life."

"From whom?"

"The police. They tried to kill both of us."

"You ran. They think you're a killer. That's what happens."

"I didn't run. I mean, not at first. I took off when I realized they were going to shoot us down in cold blood."

He didn't believe her. Not one iota. "Why would they do that?"

"I don't know." Wincing slightly, she motioned toward a chair at the small table. "Sit down."

Madrid didn't take the chair. He stood his ground and faced her. "What are you doing to do? Kill me, too?"

"I haven't killed anyone. I'm just trying to stay alive."

He watched her closely as she snagged a length of rope from the coatrack near the door. She leaned heavily against the table as she passed by it. She was shaking now. The tendrils of hair framing her face were wet and pasted to her skin. Fever, he thought. Was she sick?

"How did you find me?"

"That's what I do. I find people." He lifted a shoulder, let it fall. "It wasn't that hard." He cut her a hard look. "It's only a matter of time before the police figure out where you are."

She glanced over her shoulder at the darkened

windows beyond. In her eyes Madrid saw the worried look of a hunted animal. One that was tired and ready for the hunt to end. Good, he thought. She was exhausted and scared, that gave him an edge. He moved closer.

She turned to him abruptly, jabbed the gun at the chair. "I told you to sit down. Put your hands behind your back."

"You're not going to get away with this. Why don't you make this easy on both of us and give it up before someone gets hurt?"

"Someone already has been hurt," she snapped. "Angela is dead and for some reason unbeknownst to me, the police think I did it. Now they're trying to kill me and that innocent little boy."

She used the back of her sleeve to wipe the sweat from her forehead. Her face was so pale the skin looked translucent. Her pistol hand shook, and she blinked as if she were having a difficult time focusing.

Madrid stepped toward her. "You look like you need a doctor."

"What I need is to know why the police are trying to hang this on me and why they want to hurt that little boy."

"Let me help you figure it out."

Raising the pistol, she choked out a desperate laugh and took a step back. "Stay away from me or I swear I'll pull this trigger."

"Jessica, give me the gun."

"Don't make me use—"

He lunged at her, shoved the muzzle toward the ceiling. A cry escaped her as his fingers closed around her gun hand. A gunshot exploded, and bits of plaster floated down. She was surprisingly strong for her size, but Madrid overpowered her with ease. One twist and the gun was his. Grasping her other arm at the shoulder, he shoved her back.

"Settle down," he snapped.

She fought well, but he doubted she weighed much more than a hundred pounds soaking wet. She'd been no match for his six-foot-three frame and 180-pound bulk.

"I'm taking you in for the murder of Angela Matheson," he said.

"I didn't kill her." She staggered, using her arm against the wall to regain her balance. "You have to believe me."

"Tell it to the judge, honey." Tugging cuffs from his belt, he started toward her. "Turn around and show me your wrists."

Before he could enforce the order, she staggered again. She grasped the doorjamb to maintain her balance. But her eyes rolled back white. Her knees buckled and she reached out as if to break her fall. Then she pitched forward like a dead weight.

Chapter Two

Madrid caught her just in time to keep her from falling. He knew the faint was a ploy. A feeble attempt to regain control of the situation—or the gun. He was forced to rethink that assumption when he noticed fresh blood on the sleeve of her sweatshirt.

"Damn it," he muttered.

She was like a rag doll against him. Her skin was hot to the touch and slick with sweat. She was burning up with fever. The scent of sandalwood and sweet vanilla titillated his nostrils as he swept her into his arms. He was aware of the brush of her hair against his face and the soft curves of a very female body. Details he shouldn't be noticing about a woman who'd shot and killed a fellow agent.

Cursing, he looked around the dim interior of the cottage. The small kitchen opened to a living room, where a leather sofa was piled high with Navajo-print pillows. He carried her to the sofa, shoved the pillows aside and laid her down. At some point her sweatshirt had ridden up. As if of its own accord, his gaze flicked to an exposed midriff that was curvy and flat. He saw the silhouette of smallish breasts. Lower, the denim hugged shapely hips and slender thighs. She didn't look like a killer, but he knew from experience that looks could be deceiving.

Dragging his gaze away from details he was a fool to notice at a time like this, he tugged the sweatshirt down and tried to ascertain where the blood was coming from. Turning on the lamp beside the sofa, he knelt, located another stain on her sleeve the size of a saucer. Definitely blood.

Madrid had seen enough shootings in the course of his career to know when someone had been shot. He wondered why Mummert hadn't mentioned it. In most police departments the firing of a weapon called for at least a ream of paperwork. Had he known there was a possibility she'd been shot, Madrid would have checked area hospitals. Had one of Norm Mummert's men shot her? Or had Angela done it while trying to protect herself?

Madrid tugged the sleeve up. The knotted

gauze on her left biceps was blood soaked. From the look of it, she'd tried to bandage it herself, but hadn't been able to manage with one hand. Quickly he untied the haphazard bandage and removed it.

The bullet had grazed her, digging a trench through flesh and muscle. The wound wasn't dangerously deep, but it had bled plenty. If he wasn't mistaken, infection was setting in.

Considering what this woman had done, there was a part of him that thought she deserved whatever bad luck fate could dole out. But the human part of him hated seeing a pretty woman hurt.

She thrashed about and a moment later her eyes fluttered open, though they remained unfocused. "Didn't…do…it."

"Take it easy," Madrid said roughly.

"No." She lashed out with her fists. "Cops… tried to…kill me."

"Stay still."

"Please…don't let them…hurt Nicolas."

The reference to the boy gave him pause, but only for a second. "Where's the boy?" he asked.

"Angela asked me to…keep him safe…from the cops."

Madrid felt himself go still, wondering if

she'd just said what it sounded like. "What did you say?"

She mumbled something unintelligible that ended with the only words he could understand. "She gave me…photo."

"What photo?" he pressed. "What the hell are you talking about?"

But her eyes rolled back. She groaned and her body went slack. Frustration more than concern washed over him when she lapsed into unconsciousness.

He stared down at her, hating the fact that he wasn't going to be able to cuff her and drag her to jail by the scruff of her pretty neck. That maybe this wasn't as simple as he'd thought.

Cops…tried to…kill me.

Her words rang in his ears as he sat back on his heels and tried to decide what to do next. He told himself he shouldn't believe a word of what she'd said. The woman had shot a federal agent, assaulted a police officer, kidnapped a minor and gone on the run. She was desperate and would do anything to save herself.

But there was one thing missing: motive. Because of that he couldn't quiet the niggling little voice in the back of his mind warning him that things might not be as they appeared.

Madrid had been an agent far too long to take anything at face value. He trusted no one, he believed very little of what he was told.

But he also knew that many times delirium was like a truth serum. When people were sick out of their minds they didn't have the where-withal to lie. Especially an elaborate lie and a bullet wound to back it up.

Outside, the storm had broken. Rain lashed the roof with the same violence as the sea pounding the rocky coast. Thunder rattled the windows, and wind gusts shook the cottage. Heeding nature's message, Madrid accepted the fact that he would not be taking this woman back to the mainland tonight.

He considered calling Mummert's office to let him know he had her in custody. But something stopped him. He didn't want to acknowledge the doubt nipping at the back of his consciousness. But it was there, like a headache waiting to be reckoned with. Angela had been a top-notch agent; she'd had good instincts when it came to people. So why had she opened her door to this woman? Why had she told her about this cottage? The answer disturbed him as much as the questions themselves.

Angela had trusted Jessica Atwood.

Madrid stared down at her sweat-soaked face, the bloodstain on her shirt. All the while her words echoed hollowly in his ears.

Angela asked me to...keep him safe...from the cops.

Madrid knew better than anyone that people weren't always who they said they were; first impressions could be deceiving. After all, he was a master at deception himself. But he'd learned a long time ago to trust his instincts. He didn't like it, but right now his instincts were telling him something was amiss.

He'd wanted to end this tonight and take this woman in. He wanted her to pay for taking a life and leaving a little boy without a mother. He'd wanted to prove a point to Sean Cutter. Madrid hated it, but none of those things was going to happen as quickly as he'd wanted.

"Who the hell are you?" he whispered above the din of rain against the roof.

Recalling she'd mentioned a photo, he looked around, found nothing, then glanced down at her. Her eyes were closed, but her limbs were restless. He wondered if the photo really existed or if she'd been delirious. Or lying. Would the photo answer any of the questions zinging around in his head?

He wasn't above searching a woman, unconscious or otherwise. Especially if it might help solve the murder of a fellow agent. The sweatshirt had no pockets, but her jeans did. Frowning, he slid his hand into her front pocket and felt around. Nothing. He shifted her slightly and tried the other, found it empty. Turning her onto her side, he checked the rear pocket. His fingertip brushed something slick—plastic. He slid it from its nest. A plastic bag...with a picture inside it.

The quality was grainy, but clear enough for him to discern the dozen or so young women jammed into what looked like a small room. He removed the photo and studied it. Most of the women appeared to be of Asian descent. Some were bound, a few looked battered. All of them looked frightened.

"What the hell?"

The floor creaked behind him. He reached for the pistol he'd taken from Atwood, and swung it around. The sight of the little boy standing a few feet away hit him in the gut like a punch. He was five or six years old, tops, and wearing a pair of baggy blue jeans, a red sweatshirt and a Giants baseball cap. In his arms he clutched a stuffed hippo.

"Mah-mah."

For the first time since arriving, Madrid felt as if he were out of his element. He might be a whiz at chasing down killers, but when it came to kids he hadn't a clue. "It's okay," he whispered.

The little boy didn't acknowledge him. His eyes were fastened on the woman collapsed on the sofa. Crying out, the child ran to her, threw his arms around her and began to rock.

"Mah-mah."

Madrid watched the scene unfold. He might not know a damn thing about kids, but he knew enough about human nature. One thing was for certain—this child was not afraid of Jessica Atwood.

"What the hell is going on here?" he muttered.

The only answer he got was the pounding of rain against the roof and the uneasy sensation that nothing was as it seemed.

JESS FLOATED TO CONSCIOUSNESS one sense at a time. The first thing she became aware of was the incessant crash of the sea against the rocky shore. Then the ebb and flow of pain in her left arm. She was lying on her side with her knees pulled up to her chest.

Everything that had happened rushed back like

the memory of some terrible nightmare. Adrenaline sent her bolt upright even before her eyes were fully open. Pain in her arm wrenched a cry from her, sent her back down. For a moment she lay there, confused and fighting panic.

"Welcome back" came a low male voice.

Jess opened her eyes and found herself staring at a man with eyes the color of midnight. A day's growth of whiskers darkened his lean jaw. He was watching her with an intensity that unnerved her, the way a predator might watch injured prey seconds before pouncing.

He was the man who'd accosted her outside the cottage. She remembered struggling with him. He'd identified himself as a federal agent. But then, why wasn't she in jail? Or at the very least in a hospital bed with an armed guard posted at the door?

"You don't look like a fed," she said.

One side of his mouth curved, but his eyes remained cool, aloof. "You don't look like a killer."

She thought of Angela and closed her eyes against the quick swipe of pain. "I'm not a killer."

"Save it for some bleeding-heart jury."

"I want to see your credentials."

The sound he made was more growl than laugh.

"The last guy who identified himself as a cop tried to kill me," she added.

Scowling, he tugged a thin black wallet from his jeans and held it out for her to see. It was a photo ID—Mike Madrid. U.S. Attorney's Office.

"It's a fake," he said.

"I figured that," she returned dryly.

"I'm not with the U.S. attorney's office. I'm CIA. More specifically the MIDNIGHT Agency. The fake ID was to get me past the local PD."

"Why is the CIA involved?"

"I was hoping you could tell me." He shoved the wallet back into his pocket.

"All I know is that one of my best friends in the whole world is dead and now the police are trying to kill me."

"You expect me to believe that?"

"I don't know what to expect anymore." Jess looked around, tried to get her bearings. The windows were dark. She could hear rain lashing the roof, the sea battering the beach at the foot of the cliffs. She had no idea how long she'd been unconscious.

"How long was I out?" she ask him.

"Almost an hour." He leaned back slightly and studied her with dark, inscrutable eyes. "How did you get that bullet wound?"

"I told you. The cops tried to kill me."

"That's pretty much standard operating procedure when a murder suspect attacks a police officer and tries to run."

"I was not armed and I did not attack a cop. I ran because the cop was going to kill us." Worry trickled through her when she thought of Nicolas. "Where's Nicolas?"

"In the bedroom."

"I want to see him." When he only looked at her, she added, "Please. He's scared. He misses his mother."

"You can see him after you've answered my questions."

Hating that he had the upper hand, that she was going to have to cooperate, she struggled to a sitting position, wincing when her arm protested. That was when she realized she was no longer wearing her clothes. She glanced down at the unfamiliar T-shirt. Alarm vibrated through her, followed by a terrible sense of vulnerability. "Where are my clothes?"

"In the dryer."

"But why did you..." Not wanting to finish the sentence, she let her words trail. "You had no right to..."

"The bullet wound wasn't going to wait. It

needed to be cleaned and bandaged. You were covered with blood and mud, and frankly I couldn't see leaving you like that."

She knew it was ridiculous considering the situation, but a hot blush heated her cheeks. "I passed out?"

"That bullet wound is infected."

She already knew that; her arm throbbed with every beat of her heart.

"I found a first aid kit." He motioned to a small red-and-white kit on the coffee table. "Angela had some antibiotics from an old prescription. I would have started you on them, but I didn't know if you're allergic to penicillin."

She didn't want to take any pills, but Jess could feel the fever running hot through her body. Even if she was no longer delirious, she knew the fever was waiting at the gate for an encore. "I'm not allergic."

Never taking his eyes from hers, he uncapped a brown bottle and tapped out a capsule. "It says to take one every four hours. Let's hope this does it," he said, and handed her a glass of water.

She took the pill and drank the entire glass of water. "If you think I'm a cop killer, then why are you helping me?"

"Because I have some questions I want answered." He pulled a slip of paper from his shirt pocket. "Like where you got this."

Jess recognized the photo instantly. "You searched me, too?"

"You mentioned the photo. What did you expect?"

So much had happened in the past twenty-four hours that Jess had nearly forgotten about the photograph. She didn't understand its significance, but judging from the look in this man's eyes, he did.

"Where did you get it?" he asked.

"Angela gave it to me."

"Why? What does it mean?"

Jess closed her eyes briefly as her mind's eye took her back to the terrible moment when she'd found her friend dying on the floor in a pool of blood. Angela had been trying to speak, but she'd been so weak Jess had been able to catch only a few broken phrases. Angela had used the last of her strength to give her the photo.

"Talk to me, damn it."

His voice jerked Jess back to the present. "She gave it to me right before she died. I don't know why, and I don't know what it means. All I do know is that it was important for me to have it, because she told me to guard it and her son with my life."

Madrid stared at her the way he might a suspect who'd just lied to him. Only, Jess wasn't lying. How was she going to make him believe her?

"Did she say anything else?" he asked after a moment.

Jess didn't want to recall those terrible last minutes of her friend's life. But she knew the truth was the only thing that would exonerate her.

She looked at Madrid, wondering if she could trust him, knowing she didn't have a choice. "She told me not to trust the cops. She begged me to keep Nicolas safe. She told me to bring him here. To this cottage."

"How did she die?" he asked, his voice rough.

"She'd been shot in the abdomen." Remembering, Jess shuddered. "There was a lot of blood."

He had one of the most penetrating stares she'd ever encountered. The kind that made her feel stripped bare. She knew it was silly, but she felt as if he could see inside her head, read her most private thoughts.

"Did she say who did it?"

"No."

Madrid scrubbed a hand over his jaw. He

looked annoyed and tired, as if he'd been up all night and knew he wasn't going to sleep any time soon. "I want you to start at the beginning and tell me everything."

Jess didn't know if he was friend or foe. He had a badge that identified him as a federal agent, but considering the cops back at Lighthouse Point, she didn't know if that was good or bad. Then a little voice reminded her he'd cleaned up her bullet wound. He'd given her antibiotics. If he wanted her dead, he could have killed her a dozen times by now.

She told him her story. "Angela was letting me live in the little apartment above her garage."

"Why are you here?"

"I had some...problems. I needed a place to stay."

"What kind of problems?"

She broke eye contact. "A divorce."

He nodded. "Go on."

"I received a call at about midnight. It was Nicolas. He was keening and terrified."

"He's noncommunicative?" Madrid asked.

She nodded. "He's autistic. Even though he's five years old, he doesn't speak. He does communicate in other ways, though, with his voice and body language."

Madrid grimaced. "What happened next?"

Gooseflesh slinked down her arms as the memory rushed back. "I threw on my clothes and ran down the steps. The garage is detached, so it took me a minute or so to reach the house. When I came through the front door, I could hear Nicolas crying. I called out, but no one answered, so I went farther inside."

Images of the way Angela had looked lying on the floor in a pool of blood flashed in her mind's eye. "I found her in the kitchen. She was alive, but barely. Nicolas was hysterical and screaming. I called 911, then went to her. She kept trying to talk, but she was so weak. I didn't know how to help her."

"I want you to tell me exactly what she said. Word for word. It could be important."

Jess closed her eyes. The part of her that didn't want to remember the horror of the moment rebelled. But the part of her that knew she had to get to the bottom of her friend's death took her back.

She repeated, slowly and precisely, everything she'd already told the man. "The last thing she did was give me the photo."

"Then what happened?"

"The police arrived."

"Who, specifically?" he snapped.

"The chief," she snapped back. "Norm Mummert. And two officers."

"They arrested you on the spot?"

She shook her head. "It didn't even cross my mind that I could be a suspect. They questioned me for a few minutes. I told them exactly what had happened, and everything seemed fine. The chief asked the officer to drive Nicolas and me to the station so we could make a formal statement." The memory made her mouth go dry. "Midway to town, the cop turned on to a dirt road."

"Which cop?"

"Finks is his name, I think. Tall guy. Crew cut."

"Go on."

A tremor went through her as she recalled the drive down the isolated dirt road. "I asked him what he was doing, but he ignored me. Just kept driving. About a mile down the road he stopped and told me to get out of the car. It was incredibly dark and deserted. When I got out of the car, he drew his gun. He tried to handcuff me, but I fought him and somehow managed to break free. I grabbed Nicolas and ran."

The memory of the wild jaunt through the dark woods made her shudder. "Nicolas was exhausted and upset. He was keening and crying for Angela." She shook her head. "After a while we stopped to rest. I was scared, but I kept thinking if we could get back to the main road we could flag down a motorist and everything would be okay." She closed her eyes. "But it wasn't."

Madrid waited, his dark eyes expectant and hard.

"I thought what Finks had done was an isolated thing. A bad cop taking advantage of his position. I would have stopped and talked to the cops to straighten things out. But they never gave me the chance. They never stopped shooting."

Their eyes met, and for an instant neither of them spoke. The only sound came from the rain beating against the windows.

Jess broke the silence. "A bullet grazed my arm. I thought we were both going to die. I was bleeding, afraid I was going to end up like Angela. But I kept thinking about Nicolas, about my promise to Angela that I would keep him safe. So we kept running." She blew out a pent-up breath. "The woods were thick. The terrain had become rough. I must have stumbled over a rock or tree trunk, because the next thing I knew I was tumbling into a ravine. At first, I'd managed to hold on to

Nicolas. But by the time we hit the water below I'd lost his hand."

"You went into the water?"

She looked down at her battered hands. "The current was incredibly swift and swept me downstream. I remember debris striking me. Finally I heard Nicolas screaming and somehow managed to grab his hand. But I didn't know how badly I was injured. I was terrified I would pass out. That the cop would find us and finish what he'd begun."

"How did you end up here?" he asked.

"After a while the current slowed. I managed to grab a tree root as we passed a bridge not far from the Lighthouse Point marina. I remembered Angela telling me to bring Nicolas here, to the island. I knew she kept a boat there."

"So you stole it?"

"I did what I had to do to stay alive."

"What about the gun?" he asked.

"Angela's," she replied. "I found it here."

"That's convenient as hell."

"There's nothing convenient about any of this." She nodded toward the door where Nicolas slept. "I made her a promise, and I intend to keep it."

"Or maybe you wanted her child for yourself."

Anger swept through her with such force that she broke a sweat. "That's an absurd assumption."

"That's the chief's theory."

"He's wrong." She contemplated him for a moment, looking for some emotion that would tell her what he was thinking, what his agenda was. But his face was as unreadable as a stone. "I didn't kill her. You've got to believe me."

"I haven't decided what I believe yet."

She had. She didn't trust this man.

"You can count on one thing," he said after a moment. "I'm going to get to the bottom of this. I'm going to find the person who killed Angela. If it's the last thing I do, I'm going to make them pay."

Chapter Three

"How in the name of God did an unarmed woman and a little boy manage to elude four men armed with shotguns, two bloodhounds and a chopper equipped with infrared?" The man in the Italian-made suit and shiny wingtips paced as he snarled the words.

The rotund man standing opposite his desk shifted his weight from one foot to the other. "The terrain was rugged. It was dark and raining."

"Don't hand me excuses, damn it! Your men are supposed to be trained professionals. How do you explain this catastrophe?"

"We had a lot of ground to cover in a very short period of time."

"That doesn't change the problem we're facing."

"We believe Atwood was hit. We found blood…"

The suited man's eyes blazed with a volatile mix of fury and disbelief. "I don't want her hit! Hit people can still talk. I want her dead. And I want the child dead! I want them dead yesterday. Do you understand?"

"With all due respect, another death so soon will raise questions—"

"Atwood shot and killed a Lighthouse Point police officer. She kidnapped an autistic child. She is armed and dangerous with nothing left to lose. Believe me, her death at the hands of a police officer will not be questioned."

The man standing opposite the desk didn't look convinced.

"If Atwood talks to the wrong person she could blow this entire operation sky-high. I will not spend the rest of my life in prison because your men are incompetent."

The other man felt a drop of sweat slide between his shoulder blades. "I have four men looking for them around the clock."

"Look harder. No one disappears without a trace."

"She could have drowned in the river."

The man in the suit spun and crossed to his lackey. Sweat glistened on his face. A vein in his temple looked as if it might burst. "Do not make the mistake of assuming she drowned. She is a walking time bomb. If she talks, all of us will be going to prison for a very long time. The flow of money will come to a grinding halt. I will do whatever it takes to keep both of those things from happening. Am I clear?"

The rotund man wiped sweat from his brow. "Yes, sir."

The man in charge turned away and paced to the wall. "Use your resources to check all the local hospitals to see if any bullet wounds have been reported. Find out who her friends are. Check with family members. Pay them a personal visit. Make sure they know she is a fugitive and the full force of the law will come down on them like a ton of bricks if they do not cooperate."

"All right."

Grinding his teeth, the man crossed to the topographical map pinned to the wall. He glared at the area circled in red. He studied the river. "There's a marina at the mouth of the river."

"That's correct."

"Have you checked with the harbormaster?"

"I'll take care of it personally. Right away."

He reached out and put his hand on the other man's beefy shoulder. But the ice in his eyes belied his serene expression. "We've been good to you."

"Yes, you have."

"The benefits have been rewarding?"

"The benefits have exceeded my expectations."

"If you want things to remain that way, find the woman and the boy and eliminate them. Are we clear?"

"Crystal." The man was sweating when he left the room.

BENEATH THE YELLOW LIGHT of the banker's lamp Madrid studied the photo. The poor resolution and lighting made it difficult to make out details. Either the camera had been hidden or the photographer had been rushed. He wished for his computer and photo enhancing software. Unfortunately none of that was available, so he was going to have to make do with his naked eye.

The photo showed seventeen young women, most of Asian descent, crowded into a small, dark room. At least nine of the women were bound. Two had visible facial bruising. Were they being held against their will? If so, by whom? Where had the photo been taken?

In the background he saw what could be a

bare mattress. A beat-up bucket. There were no windows, and only one wall was visible, made of what looked to be some type of corrugated steel.

He wondered if Angela had snapped the picture from a tiny camera hidden on her person. Had this been part of her mission? Had her cover been blown and she'd been murdered before she could report back to the agency?

"What the hell were you onto?" he whispered.

The floor creaked behind him. In one smooth motion Madrid snagged the pistol off the desk and spun. Surprise rippled through him at the sight of Jessica Atwood standing at the bedroom door.

Her eyes flicked to the gun leveled at her chest and she went white. "I didn't mean to scare you."

Frowning, he set the pistol on the desk. "You'd be wise not to sneak up on a man when he's armed."

She wore an oversize T-shirt and a pair of drawstring pants she must have found in the dresser. Her feet were bare. She wasn't wearing a bra. Another thing he shouldn't be noticing.

He'd left her sleeping with Nicolas a couple

of hours earlier. He wished she'd stayed in the bedroom. She was pretty, and he didn't want her distracting him from his work.

He turned back to the photo.

"My fever broke," she said. "I'm feeling better. Clearheaded."

"The antibiotics must be working."

A pause. "What are you doing?"

Madrid didn't answer. He didn't want to engage her; he still wasn't totally convinced she was innocent. On the other hand, the more he thought about the circumstances surrounding Angela's death, the more he came to believe there was something sinister going on in Lighthouse Point. Something that went far beyond Jessica Atwood.

"Does it tell you anything?"

He turned, gave her a look he hoped conveyed his annoyance. "What?"

"The photo."

Realizing he was staring—and that she'd noticed—he tore his gaze away from her and looked at the photo. "Maybe."

"Hard to tell much with the graininess and bad lighting." She came up beside him and looked at the photo. "They look scared."

That was the first thing that had struck him,

too—the terror in the women's eyes. "I'll bet the farm they're being held against their will."

"In a place where there are no windows. No light." She leaned closer. "I don't see any doors."

He let her think aloud. "Except for where the photographer was standing. Might be a door there."

"A cave, maybe? A truck?"

"A container," he said. "Cargo."

She looked at him, nodded. "You're right."

Madrid scowled at the thought. Human smuggling was an ugly business. He knew it happened overseas. Was it possible someone was operating in the United States? He was going to have to call Sean Cutter. He only hoped the head of MIDNIGHT would tell him what he needed to know. They hadn't exactly parted on friendly terms.

"Do you think Angela stumbled upon something she shouldn't have?" Jess asked.

"I think her murder is just the tip of the iceberg. I think we're dealing with something large scale that involves a lot of very bad people."

She thought about that for a moment. "I don't understand how that involves Nicolas and me. We don't know anything."

"Are you sure about that?"

Her gaze flicked to his. Madrid steeled himself against her beauty. Against the attraction simmering low in his gut. He listened hard to the little voice telling him, *Don't go there.*

"What do you mean?" she asked.

"Are you sure Nicolas didn't see anything?"

"He can't speak."

"Maybe they're not willing to risk their lives on the possibility that one day he will, or maybe communicate what he saw."

Her eyes widened. "My God. You think he saw the murder?" Jess pressed a hand to her abdomen. "Poor little guy."

"That's just one scenario."

"What's the other?"

"Maybe they're not after Nicolas. Maybe they think Angela told you something before she died."

"Like what?"

"Like what she was onto. Names. Locations. Something damaging to them."

"She didn't."

"Her killer doesn't know that."

A tremor went through her, but her eyes took on a look of determination. Against his will he found his respect for her bumping up a notch.

"What kind of person could be so cold-blooded?" she asked.

"The kind of person ruthless enough to deal in human cargo."

"You mean smuggling?"

He lifted a shoulder, let it drop. "It's my best guess."

She absently rubbed her hand over the bandage. "We can't let them get away with what they've done."

"I don't plan on it," he said.

"What if they run?"

"If there's a container ship sitting somewhere in the United States with human cargo on board, they've already got too much invested." He gave her a hard look. "You can bet they're not going to leave two loose ends dangling."

Realization darkened her eyes. "You mean Nicolas and me."

"That's exactly what I mean."

Shaking her head, she motioned toward the door where the little boy slept. "He's already been through so much. He's an innocent kid who's just lost his mom. He doesn't deserve this."

Madrid felt something go soft in his chest. Sympathy, he realized. For a little boy who would never know his mother. For a mother who would never see her child grow up. "Do you think he'll be able to tell us anything?"

"I don't know. Angela and I were talking about it one day. She told me communication problems are common with autistic children. They tend to go inside themselves, into their own world, and Nicolas is no different."

"Can he draw? Or if we showed him photos, could he identify a killer?"

"I don't know him well enough to say." She shrugged. "All I know is that Angela loved him more than anything in the world. She worked with him daily. She'd enrolled him in a special school. She even took him to equine therapy twice a week. She was a great mom."

"Did she tell you Nicolas is gifted?" Madrid asked.

"I knew." She turned questioning eyes on him. "How do you know that? Angela didn't talk about that much."

He didn't answer. Angela had told him the last time he'd talked to her. That had been almost a year ago. Madrid wished he'd done a better job of keeping in touch.

"He plays the piano like a little fiend," she said fondly. "From chopsticks to Chopin."

"He also does high-school level math."

She turned a surprised gaze on him. "How do you know so much about Nicolas?"

"I knew Angela once," he said. "A long time ago."

"She never mentioned you."

"I'm not the kind of guy you talk about."

She contemplated him. "How did you know her?"

Because he wasn't quite sure how to answer, Madrid steered the conversation back to the topic at hand. "In any case, I think Nicolas saw something that night."

"The murder," she murmured.

"We have to find a way to reach him without traumatizing him further. The question is how."

She jumped when a gust of wind rattled a loose shutter. Madrid stared at her. Even sleep-rumpled and recovering from a fever she was pretty. Her face was as smooth and pale as porcelain, her mouth as wet and soft as some exotic tropical fruit. He wondered what she would taste like if he leaned close and brushed his mouth against hers.

Pulling himself back from a place he didn't want to go, he stood abruptly and started to walk away. "Get some sleep," he growled.

"Madrid."

He stopped, but didn't turn to her.

"Why haven't you turned me in?" she asked. "Taken me back?"

He thought about the exchange with Cutter and knew at some point he was going to have to fix things. "I like to know who the good guys are first."

"The good guys don't shoot at an unarmed woman and innocent child."

He didn't need to be reminded of that. "An innocent woman doesn't run when the police tell her to stop."

"They would have shot me on the spot. I didn't want to end up like Angela."

He turned and gave her a hard look, searching for a lie, finding none. "Get some sleep. I've got some calls to make."

Unclipping his cell phone from his belt, he turned and walked away.

MADRID LISTENED to the bedroom door close, then dialed the number from memory. Even though it was going on one o'clock in the morning in D.C., fellow MIDNIGHT operative Jake Vanderpol answered on the second ring.

"I thought it might be you," Jake growled.

"That's because I'm the only person you know who's in enough trouble to warrant a call at this hour."

"Cutter told me what happened."

"Grapevine must be busy."

He sighed. "Madrid, you screwed up big-time."

"Not the first time."

"Might be the last. Cutter is royally ticked."

"He ought to be more ticked at Angela's murderer than me."

"You know Cutter will do right by her."

"Cutter thinks this is business as usual. It's not, damn it."

"He thinks you're a loose cannon."

"Maybe I am."

"Your attitude isn't helping."

"I'm not in this to rack up points."

"Good thing, because you're not."

Silence hissed over the line for an instant. "I need a favor."

Jake groaned. "I knew that was coming."

"I need to know what Angela was working on."

Jake swore, then noisily cleared his throat. "I'm sorry about what happened to her, man. She was a good agent."

"Yeah." Madrid closed his eyes, surprised by the powerful swipe of grief. He hadn't loved her for a long time, but there had always been something between them that neither time nor distance could dull. "Cutter won't talk to me."

"Neither should I if I want to keep my job."

"I need to know what she was into, Jake."

"Maybe you ought to let Cutter handle this the way he thinks it should be handled."

"I need to do this." Madrid tried to keep the desperation out of his voice, but he didn't quite succeed. "Damn it, don't stonewall me."

Jake sighed, but the sound was fraught with resignation. "I'll do some digging, see what I can find out."

"I need to know what Angela was doing in Lighthouse Point, California. I need to know if she'd been sending reports back."

"I'll see what I can do."

"Find out everything you can on the local PD here."

"They dirty?"

"Too early to tell, but I don't like how the dots are connecting."

"I'm liking this less and less."

"And dig up everything you can find on Jessica Atwood. She's originally from Phoenix. Recently divorced. She and Angela went to college together."

"Any particular reason why you're interested in Atwood?"

"She's in this up to her neck," Madrid said.

"Hope this is worth it."

"It will be."

"I'll call you tomorrow."

"I owe you, Vanderpol."

"You can bail my ass out of the doghouse when Cutter relegates me to filing reports and answering the phone."

At that, Jake disconnected, leaving Madrid alone with his thoughts and the patter of rain against the roof.

JESS WOKE with her heart pounding hard against her ribs. She wasn't sure what had wakened her. The cottage was quiet. Dawn hadn't yet broken; the single window was still dark. She could hear the wind whipping around the eaves, the low rumble of thunder in the distance, the ping of rain against the roof.

Movement on the other side of the room sent her bolt upright. A scream hovered in her throat for an instant before she realized it was Nicolas. The little boy was at the window, rocking back and forth.

"Mah-mah," he said. "Mah-mah."

Sympathy washed over her with such force that for a moment Jess had to blink back tears. He looked so small and alone. He'd lost so much.

The need to hold him, reassure him, sent her

from the bed. At his side she knelt and put her arm around his little shoulders. "Hi, sweetie. Are you okay?"

"Mah-mah. Mah-mah."

She brushed the hair away and kissed his forehead. "What are you doing up at this hour?"

Jess didn't know much about children, even less about children with special needs. He seemed agitated, but she didn't know why. She had no idea how to calm him. "It's going to be okay, kiddo."

"Mah-mah."

She tried to gently guide him back to the bed, hoping he would sleep, but he resisted. It was as if he didn't want to leave the window. "Mah-mah. Mah-mah."

"It's okay, sweetie."

"Mah-*mah*!"

"Honey, what's wrong?"

The bedroom door flew open. A yelp escaped her as she spun. Mike Madrid stood silhouetted in the doorway, a tall, menacing figure with a gun.

His eyes flicked from her to Nicolas and back to her. "Get dressed."

The tone of his voice snapped her out of her momentary stupor. "What is it?" she asked in a low voice.

"We've got company."

For an instant she was too shocked to speak. Then the fear took hold. "Who? How did they—"

"I don't know." Crossing to the window, he parted the curtains. "Are you strong enough to run?"

"I think so." She glanced at Nicolas. "I'm not so sure about him. He seems...upset."

"I'll take him." Madrid turned to her, pulled back the slide on the pistol. "I said get dressed. Now." He turned back to the window.

Jess grabbed her clothes off the chair next to the bed. She stepped into her jeans, dragged the sweatshirt over her head. She looked wildly around for her shoes, found them near the door and jammed her feet into them.

"Where are we—"

The window shattered. Glass pelted Madrid and tinkled to the floor. Rain and wind whipped the curtains into a frenzy. He reeled back, then dropped to a shooter's stance and fired off six rapid-fire shots.

"Take Nicolas out the front," he said over his shoulder. "Run down to the beach."

Darting across the room, she took the boy's hand. He was still rocking, whimpering like a hurt animal. Through the broken window she heard shouting. She glanced at Madrid, and a fresh wave of terror enveloped her. As if in slow motion she saw him raise the pistol and fire. Someone from outside returned fire.

He swung around, his face angry. "Run, damn it! Go!"

Tightening her hold on Nicolas's hand, she sprinted toward the front door, flung it open. Rain and cold greeted her like a slap, but she barely noticed. All she cared about was getting the little boy to the relative safety of the beach.

"Come on, sweetie," she said as she took him across the deck and down the steep wooden stairs where the ocean pounded rock and sand.

She could feel the pain in her arm coming to life now, the throb keeping perfect time with the wild beat of her heart. But Jess didn't slow down.

When they reached the wide stretch of beach, the crash of the surf was deafening and salty spray dampened her clothes. The horizon was gray with the promise of dawn. She looked around, but didn't know which way to run.

Nicolas tugged her arm to the left. For an instant she debated, then went with him. The sand sucked at her shoes as she ran. The ocean roiled to her right; to her left jagged rocks jutted from the sand, offering the perfect cover for an ambush.

She was midway to a neighbor's wooden stairs when a man lunged at her from behind a rock. Jess screamed, swung around to run in the opposite direction. The gunshot that hit the sand less than a foot from them stopped her dead in her tracks.

"Stop right there or I swear I'll kill you both where you stand," said a guttural voice.

Dizzy with terror, Jess raised her hands to shoulder level and slowly turned to face the man. "What do you want?" she panted.

"I want you dead." His mouth twisted into an ugly smile as he leveled a deadly looking pistol on Nicolas. "Both of you."

"Don't hurt him," she cried. "He's just an innocent little boy."

The man looked about as sympathetic as a snake about to devour a mouse. With the gun never wavering from Nicolas, he tugged out his cell phone. "I got 'em. On the beach just south of the house." He paused. "Do you want to talk to them or do you want me to do them right here? Okay…" he said, and hung up.

Do them…

He's going to kill us, Jess thought, and her heart went wild in her chest.

The gunman's rodentlike eyes sought hers as he raised the pistol to her chest. "This ain't your lucky day," he said.

Chapter Four

Jess couldn't believe her life was going to end this way. The only decision left was whether she was going to make a run for it and take a bullet in the back or put her arms around the frightened child at her side and wait for the killing shot.

"Please don't," she said.

Beside her, Nicolas gripped her leg, keening as he rocked back and forth. *I'm sorry, Angela*, she thought. In the back of her mind she wondered where Madrid was. If he'd been shot or perhaps already killed...

Dropping to her knees, Jess put her arms around the little boy and turned her back to the man. She closed her eyes and held Nicolas tightly against her. "It's going to be all right," she whispered.

But the lie broke her heart.

A wave crashed off to her right. The wind buffeted her. At some point the rain had soaked clean through to her skin. The precious last moments of her life…

A gunshot shattered her thoughts. Jess opened her eyes to see the man with the gun crumple to the sand. A second man descended the wooden steps at a rapid clip, a gun silhouetted in his hand.

With no time to think, she grabbed Nicolas's hand, lunged to her feet and pulled him into a dead run down the beach. "Run!" she screamed. "Faster!"

She tried to keep Nicolas close to the rocks for cover. The sand hindered her, but she plowed through.

"Jess!"

Somewhere in the back of her mind it registered that someone had called her name. But she was operating on pure terror and the primal will to survive. A glance over her shoulder told her the man was gaining on them.

Oh, dear God, he's going to catch us!

"Stop!"

She screamed when a heavy hand came down on her shoulder. Spinning in midstride, she let go of Nicolas's hand and shoved the boy away. "Run!"

Hoping the little boy understood, she faced her attacker and lashed out with her fists. "Get away from me!" she screamed.

The man took her down into the sand. "Easy! It's me. Madrid."

The cloak of terror lifted and Jess stopped fighting. Breathing hard, she looked up at the man on top of her. At some point she had begun to cry, huge choking sobs ripping from her throat. "He was going to—"

"He didn't." Madrid eased off her and went to his knees beside her in the sand. "Take it easy."

"He was going to kill us." Jess knew it was silly, considering she'd just cheated death, but she couldn't stop crying. "He was going to kill that innocent little boy."

"You're okay now." Madrid reached for her and they rose together.

"Where's Nicolas?"

"He's right here. He's fine."

Another sob squeezed from her throat when the little boy grabbed her leg and held on. "Are there more of them?" Setting her hand against Nicolas's soft hair, she looked around.

"No."

"Oh God, Madrid, I was so scared."

"You're safe now. Both of you."

It seemed only natural when he took her into his arms. His body was solid and warm against hers. Vaguely she was aware of him pulling Nicolas to them. The little boy was keening. Jess had one arm around Madrid. She put the other on Nicolas's shoulder and squeezed gently.

"You're going to be all right," Madrid said.

But Jess didn't feel as if she was going to be all right ever again.

MADRID WASN'T EXACTLY sure what had happened on the beach a few minutes ago, but he couldn't get it out of his mind. Even when Angela's boat was nearly swamped by five-foot swells on the way back to the mainland, he found himself thinking about the way Jess had felt in his arms. He didn't know what he was going to do about it. Nothing, if he was smart. But Madrid had never claimed to be smart when it came to women in danger.

The one thing he did know was that they needed to find out who was trying to murder Jess and Nicolas. He knew they would be back to finish the job. He'd have to figure out the rest of it later.

Instead of returning to the marina where Angela had kept the *Riptide* in a slip, he headed south, where the beach was less rocky and he could ground the boat without fear of shattering the hull.

"Where are we going?"

He looked up to see Jess and Nicolas huddled at the rear of the boat. He'd found a slicker earlier and Jess had wrapped the boy in it. Not that it helped much. All three of them were soaked to the skin. The wind was out of the northwest and the chill factor hovered somewhere around the forty-degree mark.

"We're going to ditch the boat and go ashore," he said.

"How do we know they won't be waiting for us?"

He didn't like it that her teeth were chattering, that she was wet and exposed. It wouldn't take long for hypothermia to set in. "We don't." But their pursuers were resourceful; it wouldn't be long before they caught up.

Giving Nicolas a kiss on top of his wet head, Jess rose and crossed to Madrid. "We've got to get this child to a warm and safe place," she said. "He's been through a terrible ordeal. He's cold and frightened and—"

"I know," Madrid snapped. He hated seeing the little boy so ashen and silent, especially after losing his mother. The problem was he wasn't sure what to do about it.

"There has to be someone."

Madrid knew someone. The problem was he didn't want to put that person in danger. But the way things were going, he didn't think he had a choice. "I have a place in mind."

Dawn broke with a mosaic of pastels on the western horizon. Madrid steered the open fisherman south through heavy surf, then cut east toward the beach when he saw the old fishing pier. Using the pier as cover, he beached the boat. He stepped into knee-high water and helped Jess and Nicolas from the boat, then picked up the satchel of items he'd collected at Angela's place.

"What's in the bag?" Jess asked.

"Let's just say Angela was a firm believer in keeping resources handy."

Her brows went together. "If it's food you're hoarding, Nicolas could use—"

"It's not food," Madrid cut in. "That's all you need to know."

"Fine."

They trudged through sand toward the coastal road a hundred yards away. "I need to get Nicolas into some dry clothes."

Looking back at him, Madrid noticed Nicolas's teeth were chattering like little jackhammers. When they caught up with him, Madrid stooped and took the boy into his arms. "My body heat will help keep him warm."

Jess blinked at him. "Good."

Even cold and wet and frightened she was pretty. Against her pale complexion her eyes were dark and her lips were beginning to turn blue. He couldn't stop thinking about how good she'd felt in his arms.

Berating himself for dwelling on something he had no business dwelling on, he turned right at the highway toward the small fishing village of Rocky Fork half a mile down the road. Madrid wasn't sure if he would be welcomed there; he hadn't exactly left on good terms some eleven years earlier.

But with an injured woman and a child in need of shelter and food, he couldn't think of anywhere else to go. He only hoped they didn't turn him away at the door.

BY THE TIME THEY REACHED Rocky Fork, Jess was ready to collapse with exhaustion and cold. Her arm throbbed with every beat of her heart. Next to her, holding Nicolas, Madrid looked neither cold nor tired. The one thing she didn't miss was the wariness in his eyes and the fact that he looked over his shoulder every couple of minutes. It was enough to keep her going.

"You think they'll be back?" she asked.

"I think it's only a matter of time." He motioned toward an old stone church and they took the cobblestone walkway toward the rear.

"Why are we stopping here?"

"I know a guy" was all he said.

At the rear of the building Madrid shoved open a heavy wood door and held it for Jess. She stepped inside.

The interior of the old church was dimly lit, but warm. Scents of incense and candle wax floated in the air. Beyond the small nave and old-fashioned pews stood the altar, framed by stained glass windows that rose twenty feet into the air.

"Welcome to St. Augustine. May I help you?"

Jess spun to see a tall man approach. The darkness of his hair and eyes was echoed in his slacks and jacket. She never would have pegged him as a priest, but the collar gave him away.

His friendly smile faded when he spotted Madrid, and for a moment the two men looked very much alike.

"Surprised to see me?" Madrid asked.

"I'm surprised you're still alive," said the priest.

"It hasn't been easy." Madrid extended his hand. "I need your help."

"Of course you do." But the other man accepted the handshake. "That's the only time I see you. When you need something or when you're bleeding."

"This time it's not about me."

The priest's eyes flicked to Jess, then to Nicolas. "What have you gotten yourself into now?"

"I'll fill you in later." Madrid turned to Jess. "Matt, this is Jessica Atwood. Jess, this is my brother, Father Matthew Madrid."

For a moment Jess was so shocked she couldn't speak. Of all the things she'd expected, this was not it. Trying to hide her surprise, she extended her hand. "Hello."

The other man took it, squeezed it. He had the warmest, most open smile of any man she'd ever met. "Welcome to St. Augustine." Father Matthew motioned toward Nicolas. "And the boy?"

"Angela's."

"Ah. How is she?"

Madrid's face darkened. "She's dead."

"I'm sorry." Father Matthew looked taken aback. "How—"

"Is there some place we can talk? Get dry?" Madrid glanced toward the door, a motion that was not lost on his brother.

The priest hesitated.

"Please." Jess reached out and touched the priest's arm. "Nicolas needs dry clothes and something to eat."

"Of course." Father Matthew motioned toward a door to the right of the chancel rail. "There's an old rectory that's not being used."

He led them through a courtyard to a quaint stucco building not much bigger than a single-car garage. The combined living room and kitchen had old, but functional furniture and the place smelled of dust and air freshener, but it was warm and dry and at the moment Jess couldn't think of any place more inviting.

"There are towels in the hall closet," Father Matthew said. "Blankets on the bed. Extras in the closet."

"Thank you," Jess said.

Father Matthew smiled. "You're welcome."

Madrid crossed to him and shoved several bills into his hand. "Can you get us some food?"

The two brothers' eyes met. "You owe me an explanation."

"You'll get it."

"I know what kind of lifestyle you lead, Mike. I'm not condemning it, but there are women and children here. I don't want them in danger."

"No one knows we're here." He grimaced. "We won't stay long."

Father Matthew's eyes went to Jess, and he nodded solemnly. "We'll talk later," he said, and let himself out.

JESS FELT ALMOST HUMAN after a hot shower. After rebandaging her arm, which looked much better thanks to Angela's antibiotics, she emerged to find that Madrid had washed their clothes. Afterward, she bathed Nicolas, and then the three of them sat at the small kitchen table and feasted on the hot soup and sandwiches Father Matthew had brought them.

"We need to talk."

Jess was sitting next to Nicolas, watching him play with a toy truck Father Matthew had brought him, when Madrid's voice came at her from behind. Giving the boy a kiss on top of his head, she rose and turned to Madrid. He seemed incredibly tall, and she resisted the urge to look away as his dark eyes searched hers. "All right," she said.

He motioned to the kitchen table where two cups of coffee sat steaming. "It's instant."

"As long as it's hot." She took a final look at Nicolas, then walked to the table and sat. "It was nice of your brother to take us in."

Madrid smiled. "He got the good genes."

"He knows you have a dangerous job."

He took the chair opposite her. "He's saved my ass on more than one occasion."

"What he said about endangering the children—"

He cut her off. "That's what I want to talk to you about."

Jess sensed she wasn't going to like what he said next.

"I need to work," he began. "I want you and Nicolas to stay here with Father Matthew."

"No." The word was out before she could consider the repercussions. But Jess didn't have to think about it. There was no way she could walk away from this after everything that had happened.

"Nicolas has been through enough." He glanced toward the little boy. "He needs normalcy. A routine. He's not going to get that with me."

"Those things were taken away from him the night someone put a bullet in his mother," Jess snapped.

"You're the only adult he knows. He needs you here with him."

"He can stay with Father Matthew for a few days," she said. "At least until we figure this out."

"Jess, this may take more than a few days. My brother is a stranger to him."

"Madrid, don't try to manipulate me using that child. I have to get to the bottom of this. Damn it, my life is on the line. I have far too much at stake to hand everything over to you."

"I'm a trained professional."

"Then why haven't you called in your superiors to help you on this?" she shot back.

His jaw went taut. An emotion Jess couldn't quite decipher flashed in his eyes. Surprise? Regret? It was gone before she had a chance to identify it.

"I'll contact my superiors when I have something significant to take to them."

"I'm not going to hide out here at this mission and do nothing, while I'm painted a killer and fugitive. In case you haven't made the connection, I'm the number-one suspect in Angela's murder. Evidently the cops think I'm armed and dangerous, because they're shooting first and asking questions later."

"Or maybe they want you out of the way."

That stopped her, but only for an instant. "All the more reason for me to stay involved and get to the bottom of this."

"You can't do that if you're dead!" he shouted.

"I don't plan on getting myself killed."

"Like anyone does." A sigh hissed between his tight lips. "Damn it."

"Madrid, please don't lock me out. I've been accused of murdering my best friend and kidnapping her son. There are people trying to kill me and I don't know why. If I can't clear my name, I'll be running the rest of my life."

Cursing, he rose abruptly and strode to the sink to stare out the window. The rain had stopped, but the day remained dreary and damp.

"What we need is a plan," she said after a moment.

"I have a plan." He turned back to her, gave her a hard look. "It doesn't include you."

"Then change it so that it does."

"Jess, damn it, it's dangerous."

She stared at him, wondering if he didn't want her involved because he was concerned about her safety or because he thought her incapable. "It's even more dangerous not to do anything." When he didn't speak, she went to him. "I've never been one for sticking my head in the sand. Madrid, I *need* to do this. Please. If I can help, let me help."

Growling beneath his breath, he went back to the table and sat. "I've been running everything that's happened through my head. Everything goes back to the Lighthouse Point PD."

She took the chair across from him. "I agree."

"They're hiding something."

"Something Angela found out about. Something she saw. Something Nicolas saw." She bit her lip. "Something involving that photo?"

Madrid's gaze latched on to hers. "If you were a cop and you had something to hide, where would you keep it?"

"The safest place I could think of." Jess felt a prickly sensation on the back of her neck. "Safe deposit box. Home safe."

He shook his head. "The police station."

Her eyes widened as realization dawned. "You want to break in to the police station?"

He stared at her, saying nothing.

Jess choked out an incredulous laugh. "That's suicidal."

"Do you have a better suggestion?"

"It might be more expedient to just put a pistol to our heads."

"Too bloody." He smiled, but there was little humor to it.

"You're right about one thing," she said.

He arched a brow.

"Your brother got the better genes."

"The smarter ones, anyway." But then he sobered. "Jess, I think the Lighthouse Point PD is into this up to their crew cuts."

"Into what?"

He tapped the photo Angela had given her. "Whatever this is."

She stared at the photo for a moment, then at Madrid. "What about Angela's house?"

"What about it?"

"If she had stumbled onto something at the police department, surely she would have made notes or written something down."

"I thought of that. If the cops are in on this, they've probably already gone through everything. They probably have the house staked out."

"We're considering breaking in to the police station and you're worried about a little stake-out?" she asked dryly.

"I'm mainly worried about getting shot. In case you're not up on the science of a 9 mm piece of lead penetrating the human body at two hundred miles an hour, it can be fatal."

Even though he'd said it in a dry tone, she shivered.

"I'll find a way into Angela's house first." He leaned back in the chair, set it back on two rear legs.

"That sounded singular."

"It was."

"I lived in the apartment above Angela's garage for three weeks, Madrid. I know my way around."

"I can figure it out."

"I know a way in where you can't be seen from the street."

"I'm not going to have this conversation with you." He rose, but she reached out, grasped his arm and stood, as well.

He blinked at her, then something hot flashed in his eyes. Suddenly she was aware of how hard the muscles in his arm felt beneath her fingertips. How energy ran like electricity through his body and into hers. She felt it all the way to her bones.

She didn't want to acknowledge it, but her heart was pounding. A response that had nothing to do with sneaking into police stations and everything to do with the man standing so close she could feel the heat coming off his body.

She dropped her hand from his arm. "I know how to get in without being seen."

He contemplated her with cool dark eyes. "Okay. I'll bite."

"Only if we go in together."

"Damn it, Jess." Sighing, he scraped a hand over his jaw. Jess heard the chafe of his heavy beard, realized that he hadn't shaved. That his hair smelled of pine needles. That his muscles were like steel...

"Th-there's a cellar door on the north side of the house."

"I noticed it."

"Then you know there's a hedge that runs from the back fence to the door. The lock is broken on the cellar door."

"How do you know that?"

"Because Angela and I were doing some yard work one day and she was complaining about having to fix it."

"Can you get into the house through the basement?"

Jess nodded. "There's no lock on the basement door."

She could tell she had his attention now, so she kept going. "Angela kept a home office in a downstairs bedroom. There's a file cabinet there she kept locked."

"Do you know what's inside?"

"All I know is that one night I went in to say good-night to her and she seemed...secretive about it."

He didn't look surprised and Jess got the feeling that there was more going on than she was being told. What was he hiding from her?

"I get the feeling none of this comes as a surprise to you," she said.

"I didn't know about the cellar door."

But you know why Angela kept a hidden file, a suspicious little voice added. "What aren't you telling me?"

"A lot."

She hadn't expected him to say that. She stared at him, her pulse ratcheting, her mind beginning to run through possibilities. "What?"

He motioned toward the chair. "Sit down."

Jess took the chair again, wondering what he was going to hit her with next.

"Angela was not a police officer," he said.

"What?"

"She was posing as a cop, but it was only an assignment."

"What are you talking about? What kind of assignment?"

"She was working undercover for the same

agency I work for. It's called the MIDNIGHT Agency. We're federal. Part of the CIA."

"Angela was a federal agent?" She couldn't quite get her mind around the notion. "What was she doing in Lighthouse Point?"

"I don't know. Her mission was covert. But I think she was working on something big."

Jess's head reeled with the information. "Why can't you call the agency you work for and ask for their help?"

His gaze dropped to the tabletop. "When I found out about her death, I went to my superior and asked to be assigned the case. He refused, citing the fact that I was too personally involved."

Another surprise tossed at her like a glass of ice water. "Are you?" she asked, wondering not for the first time about his relationship with Angela.

"No." He grimaced. "But my superior argued the point. Things got heated. I lost my temper."

"You quit?"

"I caught the first flight west to find her killer. No holds barred."

The way he said it made Jess shiver. She stared at him, the knowledge that two days ago he'd thought *she* was Angela's killer churning inside her.

He looked at her as if he'd read her thoughts. "I know you didn't kill her."

Relief swept through her with such power that for an instant she couldn't speak.

He continued. "You were at the wrong place at the wrong time. A corrupt police department used that to their advantage."

"To cover up a murder."

He nodded. "You're nothing more than a scapegoat."

"Do you think someone figured out Angela was a federal agent?"

Madrid shook his head. "I think someone realized she was on to their secret."

"What secret?"

"That's what we're going to find out."

Chapter Five

Madrid hadn't wanted to involve his brother, but he needed a safe haven for Nicolas while he and Jess returned to Lighthouse Point. Father Matthew wasn't happy about the arrangement, but he was too good a man to refuse Madrid help, and he would never turn a child away from his church.

"How long will you be?" he asked.

"I don't know."

Father Matthew motioned with his eyes toward Jess. "What about her?"

Madrid risked a look at Jess. Sitting on the floor, she had her arm around Nicolas's thin shoulders and was holding a little purple hippo. Nicolas had gone into his own little world, but it didn't deter Jess from talking to him, from reaching out to him.

"She's coming with me."

Father Matthew's usually serene expression turned incredulous. "I don't have to tell you that's a bad idea, do I?"

"No."

"You don't exactly have the best track record when it comes to women and decision making."

Because Madrid couldn't dispute that, he said nothing.

As if realizing he'd overstepped, Father Matthew sighed. "What can I do to help?"

"I could use a vehicle."

"I have one. It's not much, but it runs."

"That'll do."

"Anything else?"

Setting his hand on his brother's shoulder, Madrid smiled. "You might say a prayer."

MADRID WAITED UNTIL midnight before entering the Lighthouse Point city limits. His brother's car was a nondescript compact, but Madrid stuck to the back streets anyway. On the outside chance some cop would notice it and run the plates, he'd switched plates with a wrecked car he'd found parked at a service station. The last thing he wanted was for some killer to discover his brother was involved.

In the passenger seat beside him Jess sat

quietly, watching the waterlogged landscape speed by. She'd been quiet since leaving the church an hour earlier. He could tell she hadn't wanted to leave Nicolas behind. She wouldn't admit it, but he knew from the way her hands were knotted in her lap that she was nervous. Maybe even scared. He couldn't blame her; he was, too.

He wished he hadn't brought her along. He enjoyed her company, and in all honesty she would probably be some help once they got into the police station. His biggest fear was that the situation would become dangerous. It was his responsibility to make sure that didn't happen.

He glanced away from the road. "You okay?"

She started at the sound of his voice, tried to mask her jumpiness with a too quick smile. "I was just thinking about Nicolas."

"He'll be all right," Madrid said. "My brother is a natural with kids."

"It's just that he's been through so much."

"Matt will take good care of him, Jess."

She shot him a grateful smile. "I guess I should be thinking about how we're going to pull this off."

"I thought we'd check out Angela's house first. See what we can find. We can park down from the alley and go in the back way, behind the hedge."

She nodded, all business now.

When they neared Angela's house, he circled the block three times looking for cop cars, but there weren't any in sight.

"Doesn't look like they posted a sentry," Jess said.

"That doesn't mean some beefed up kid armed with a .45 isn't going to show up once we get inside."

"We'll just have to be on the lookout. Be careful."

"To say the least." Madrid punched out the headlights, turned into the mouth of the alley down the block from Angela's house and parked behind a small garage, out of sight from the street. "We walk the rest of the way."

Jess reached for the door handle.

"Wait." Before Madrid even realized he was going to move, he reached out and grasped her arm.

She turned to him. Even in the semidarkness of the car, her beauty moved him in a way he hadn't been moved for a very long time. She'd pulled her hair back and her face was a pale oval. Her eyes searched his. He could see moisture on her lips.

"I've got to douse this overhead light," he said, his tongue suddenly thick.

"Oh."

But for the span of several tense seconds neither of them moved. His hand was still on her arm. Through the material he could feel her trembling. She was scared, he thought, and felt a sharp swipe of guilt for putting her in this situation.

"You're shaking," he whispered.

"It's not like I do stuff like this every day."

"Probably a good thing."

It was a silly moment, but they smiled at each other. Madrid felt something go soft in his chest when she licked her lips. He knew he was about to make a mistake. But with the adrenaline humming and an attraction he could no longer deny heating his blood, he didn't care.

Tightening his grip on her arm, he leaned close and claimed her mouth with his. Her lips were incredibly soft and warm and moist. Madrid had kissed plenty of women in his time, but no kiss had ever affected him like this one. He could feel the need tugging at him, desire pooling low and burning hot. The urge to put his arms around her and pull her close taunted him. But he knew if he wasn't careful he was going to fall headlong into this and lose focus.

Her eyes were wide and surprised when he pulled away. Her breathing had quickened, her nostrils flaring with each breath. "Why did you do that?" she asked.

"Luck." Reaching up, he opened the overhead light cover and popped out the tiny bulb. "Ready?"

"Uh...yeah."

He opened the door. "Slide out this side."

Then they were standing next to the car. Drizzle made the night cold and damp and caused halos to form around the sodium-vapor street lamp.

"Stay low and follow me." Taking her hand, he ducked and ran toward the gate that would take them into Angela's yard.

JESS'S HEART WAS POUNDING hard as she watched Madrid fumble with the latch. The gate squeaked open and a moment later they were sprinting alongside the hedge toward the rear of the house. He paused at the cellar door and for the span of several heartbeats they listened.

"So far, so good," he whispered, and reached for the cellar door handle.

The hinges creaked as the door opened.

Narrow stairs before they descended into total
darkness. A shiver swept through her at the
thought of going down there. Back at the church,
it had seemed like a good idea. The best way to
find Angela's killers and bring them to justice.
Now staring down into the cold darkness of the
cellar, Jess suddenly wasn't so sure.

She jolted when Madrid touched her hand.
"I'll go first," he said.

"I was hoping you'd say that."

The steps creaked like old bones as he descended into the inky-black abyss. Closing her
eyes briefly, she took a fortifying breath and
followed. The smell of must and wet dirt filled
her nose. She could hear their shoes against old
wood and feel the hard thrust of adrenaline-
rich blood through her veins.

She jumped when Madrid closed the cellar
door overhead, plunging them into total
darkness. "I can't see a thing," she whispered.

"That's the idea."

Relief swept through her when the tiny beam
of a flashlight cut through the black. "You're
not scared of the dark, are you?" he asked.

"Only when I'm expecting someone with a
gun to jump out."

He took her hand, and they crossed the damp

floor and headed toward the steps that would take them to the utility room off the kitchen. "Let's make this quick."

He released her hand at the top of the stairs and pulled an ugly-looking pistol from his waistband before stepping into the utility room. Dim light from the kitchen window beyond made it possible to see. On familiar ground now, Jess started toward the door, but Madrid hooked his finger in the collar of her shirt and pulled her back.

"Let's make sure we don't have company before we start prancing around."

"I was just going to suggest that."

"Right." With the gun leading the way, he moved into the kitchen.

Jess followed. The familiar homeyness struck her as they moved through the house, clearing each room as they went. She thought of Angela, reminded herself why they were there, and the sense of purpose bolstered her. Within just a few minutes, they had established that they were alone.

"You mentioned an office," Madrid said. "That might be a good place to start."

Jess took him to the office Angela had set up in one of the extra bedrooms. A two-drawer file cabinet squatted in the corner, and a desk sat adjacent the single window, facing the door.

"You take the desk," Madrid said. "I'll take the file cabinet."

Jess went to the desk and sat in the chair. "What are we looking for?"

"Anything even remotely interesting or suspicious," he said. "Notes. Documentation. Photos. Anything that looks like code."

Jess tried the first drawer, but it was locked. Madrid must have noticed, because before she could speak he nudged her aside. In less than a minute he picked the lock.

"You're good at that," she said, amazed.

His dark gaze met hers. "I'm good at a lot of things."

You're certainly good at kissing. The errant thought came out of nowhere. She banked it quickly, but not before she felt a hot blush creep into her cheeks.

"Good at getting into trouble," she said.

"That, too." He went back to the file cabinet and began picking the lock.

Jess's pulse was racing when she looked down at the opened desk drawer. Only this time it didn't have anything to do with the fear of discovery and had everything to do with the dark-eyed man who'd kissed her as she'd never been kissed before.

Trying to get her focus back, she pulled out the first file and paged through it. Credit card bills. Utility bills. Bank statements. She closed the folder, shoved it back into the drawer and went to the next. Vaguely she was aware of Madrid doing the same thing in the file cabinet, and of rain pounding against the roof and the windows on the west side of the house.

She found a file marked "Nicolas" and opened it. Grief struck her hard at the sight of his progress reports, letters from teachers and psychologists. At the rear of the folder she found several crude drawings the little boy had done in crayon. One depicted a mother and child walking through a forest, hand in hand. Jess's throat tightened.

Oh, Angela...

"Find something?"

She started at the sound of Madrid's voice and looked up to see him standing over her shoulder, gazing at the drawing. "Just this," she said.

He grimaced, looking away. "That's a good reminder as to why we're here."

"I thought so, too." Sliding the drawing back into the drawer, she went to the next file. "I've got one more drawer to go through."

He motioned to the file cabinet. "I didn't find anything, but we still have the rest of the house." He started toward the door, but hesitated, then turned to her. "Will you be all right here?"

"Just don't get out of screaming distance."

Never taking his eyes from hers, he crossed to her and handed her the flashlight. "Keep the beam down in case someone drives by."

"Thanks." She took the flashlight.

"I'm going to poke around. I'll meet you back here in five minutes."

"Be careful," she said.

He gave her a reckless smile and then he was gone.

Jess was thinking about the kiss again as she opened the last drawer. She knew they were dangerous thoughts floating through her head; there was no way the spark that had been ignited between them could go anywhere.

"Except away," she muttered, pulling out another file.

Setting the flashlight on the desktop, she began paging through the folder. She found car insurance documents, warranties for the washing machine. A repair bill for the furnace. She was about to slide the folder back into the drawer when she came to a second one tucked inside the first. She opened it to find a small leather-bound notebook. She saw handwritten notes detailing events, dates and names.

Thursday, January 20. Finks left house a few minutes before midnight. Tried to follow—took off. Did he recognize the car? Not sure what he's up to. Suspicious. Run a background check.

Tuesday, January 25. Followed Finks. Pulled over by LPPD. Officer Styles. They know I'm up to something. Talk to Cutter tomorrow.

Sunday, January 30. Working a double shift. Watched house. Finks left at midnight. Shipyard on Luna Bay. Gate locked. Smuggling drugs? Guns? Tried to feel out Mummert. He's ready to retire. Doesn't have a clue.

Wednesday, February 2. Got in s.y. Got pics. Young women. Poor conditions. They know I know. Need proof. Gotta call Cutter and get out.

Jess knew immediately she'd discovered something important. The notes implied the Lighthouse Point PD was into something illegal, but what? Had Angela been spying on her fellow cops? Had they found out about it?

Jess paged through the folder with renewed enthusiasm. She found more notes. Photographs. A photocopy of a newspaper story. She was so involved in her work she didn't notice the play of headlights over the window until it was too late.

Chapter Six

Jess's gaze flew to the window, her heart hammering. Light flashed on the wall above her and she could see the glare of headlights through the sheer curtains. A car had pulled into the driveway. Adrenaline and fear jolted her so hard she nearly dropped the file.

"Madrid!" she whispered. "Someone's—"

She nearly yelped when his voice sounded directly behind her. "I'm right here."

She swung around to see him already darting to the window. "What do we do?" she asked.

"The official term for it is hide." Spinning away from the window, he took her hand and hauled her toward the door. "You know the house better than I do. Any suggestions?"

Possibilities spun through her mind, but fear was jumbling her thoughts. How many times had she played hide-and-seek with Nicolas?

Where did he like to hide? "Th-the staircase. There's an alcove beneath it."

He took her in that direction just as keys rattled in the front door. As the door squeaked open they ducked behind an old desk Angela had been refinishing. For a terrible moment Jess thought they had been spotted.

"Easy," Madrid whispered.

Jess barely heard him over the wild beat of her heart. She looked at him, but didn't dare speak. Someone was in the house; she could hear them moving around. Ten feet away a flashlight beam cut through the darkness, swept over the desk they were hiding behind.

Oh, God. Oh, God!

She heard heavy footfalls on the wood floor. Getting closer. Her pulse roared like a jet engine in her ears. She couldn't remember if she'd closed the desk drawer in Angela's office. Would they notice?

Closing her eyes tightly, she clutched the file against her chest and tried desperately to control her breathing. Vaguely she was aware of the crackle of a police radio.

"This is 1452. I'm 10-23, and there's no sign of a 10-14. Over."

"Roger that, 1452."

Jess opened her eyes to see the flashlight beam cut toward the kitchen. The sound of footsteps faded. Next to her, Madrid was as silent and still as stone. But she could feel the minute tremor that ran through him; she could feel the heat emanating from his body into hers, and at that moment the sensation comforted her in a way nothing else could have.

"Shhh...easy."

His mouth was less than an inch from her ear, so close she could feel the warm brush of his breath against her skin. The moment shouldn't have been anything but terrifying. It certainly shouldn't have been intimate. But even frightened for her life, Jess couldn't deny the slice of heat low in her belly.

After several minutes the front door opened and closed. The faint sound of an engine starting sounded from outside. Madrid moved out from behind the desk first. Jess straightened, but her legs were too weak to move.

He crossed to the window and peered out. "He's gone."

She pressed a hand to her stomach, the reality of what they'd narrowly avoided making her feel sick. "How did he know we were here?"

"He didn't." Madrid's eyes cut to hers. "If

he'd known he would have looked harder. He would have found us."

"But why was he here?"

He glanced out the window again. "I don't know. Maybe a neighbor saw our flashlight. Thought we were burglarizing the place." His gaze flicked to the folder she was clutching to her chest. "What's that?"

Jess had nearly forgotten about the file. "I think I found something."

He reached for it, tucked it into his waistband. "Let's get the hell out of here."

MADRID WASN'T EASILY shaken; he'd been through too many life-and-death situations to let the incident at Angela's house shake him. Only, this one had. And the response troubled him. He knew it wasn't because he feared for his own safety, but for Jess's.

He couldn't let himself get too close to her. He sure as hell couldn't let himself care. Bad things happened to the people who got close to him. Too bad he was failing miserably on both counts.

"Where are we going?"

He glanced at Jess, felt the knot in his gut loosen at the sight of her. She was lovely, and for an instant he wanted to reach out and touch her just to make sure she was real.

"In case you've forgotten, we've got one more stop to make," he said.

She looked a little green around the gills. "The police station."

"You got a better idea?"

"No."

She was trying to be brave about it, but he could tell the thought terrified her. To be perfectly honest it terrified him, too. But for all the wrong reasons.

"Look," he said, "I'm going to pull over so I can take a look at this file. Maybe there's something here that will tell us what to look for at the station." He knew it was wishful thinking, but he was hoping there was something inside the file that would clear up the mystery so they didn't have to venture into the police station at all. Not bloody likely.

"There's a dirt road up ahead," she said.

Heavy fog had moved in from the bay, giving the forest that ran along the coastal highway an ethereal appearance. Madrid turned onto a narrow dirt road. He stopped out of sight from the highway and shut down the engine. "Okay, let's see what we've got."

Jess handed him the file. "There are notes and photographs."

Turning on the dome light, he opened the file. A smile touched his mouth at the sight of Angela's neat handwriting. She'd always been meticulous. How ironic that he would appreciate that most after her death.

He read the notes twice, trying to decipher the abbreviations and read between the lines.

"Looks like she was spying on the Lighthouse Point PD," Jess said.

Madrid read the notes again, his focus lingering on the names. "She seems suspicious of Finks."

"The officer?"

He flipped to the photographs. They were similar to the one Angela had given Jess. Young women, most of Asian descent, being held against their will. The questions were *where?* and *why?*

"I still think we could be dealing with a human smuggling ring," he said after a moment.

Jess blinked at him. "It's difficult to believe things like that can happen in the United States."

"You'd be surprised by what happens in the United States."

"How does it work?"

"It's an ugly business. Young women, usually

living in impoverished conditions, are promised a better life here in the United States. Sometimes they're told they can do domestic work to repay the cost of transportation to the United States, which is usually by ship. Of course the organizer charges a fee for taking the risk and putting it all together. Usually the fee is so high these women will never be able to pay it back."

"Indentured servants."

"In essence." Madrid grimaced. "Once they arrive, they're sold to the highest bidder or sold into prostitution."

"But why don't they go to the police?"

"Because they're illegal immigrants. Most of them don't know English. They don't know their way around. They have no friends or family here. They're lied to from the moment they arrive." He rolled his shoulder. "A few escape only to wind up on the street. Most don't."

"That's incredibly sad."

"It is," he agreed. "Especially for the women who have children."

Jess looked out the window. Madrid saw her blink rapidly, knew she was thinking about Nicolas. "If the Lighthouse Point PD is involved, we have to expose them."

"I know."

The problem was Madrid wasn't quite sure how to go about it. If he'd been operating alone he'd already have come down on the Lighthouse Point PD so hard and fast they wouldn't know what had hit them. He would have taken advantage of the myriad resources he had access to through the MIDNIGHT Agency.

But nothing was going right this time. He'd estranged himself from the agency, so he couldn't call upon them for help. At least, not officially.

More important, he didn't want to put Jess in danger. He wished he'd been able to convince her to stay back at the mission with his brother. If something happened to her...

"How are we going to get inside the police department?"

He frowned at her, not liking the question, but liking very much what he saw when he looked into her eyes. Damn, he wished she hadn't come along.

"We create a diversion," he said.

Her eyes narrowed. "You have something in mind?"

"I always have something in mind." He slid the photos back into the file and put the file under the seat.

"Perhaps you could enlighten me."

"Arson," he said.

"Arson?" She gaped at him. "You mean as in breaking the law? Burning something down? What kind of agent are you?"

"The kind who knows how to get the job done."

She sighed. "What are we burning down?"

"There's a new police station and city hall being built on the south side of town. Right now it's just being framed. Lots of wood."

"A fire waiting to happen."

He lifted a shoulder, let it drop. "Part of the roof is up, so it should be partially dry."

She seemed to think about that for a moment. "What if someone gets hurt?"

"It's a stand-alone building."

"How do we go about it?"

"Leave that me," he said, and started the engine.

JESS HAD KNOWN unraveling the mystery behind Angela's murder wasn't going to be easy. But she'd been so intent on bringing the culprits to justice that she hadn't considered the dangers.

Her heart pounded hard in her chest as Madrid idled slowly past the skeletal structure of the new Lighthouse Point Police Department. The building was just off the main drag, nestled between a vacant lot and a small park. She'd driven past the place a dozen times and never given it more than a passing glance.

He parked in a narrow alley a block away, out of sight from the street, and shut down the engine. Jess watched as he reached into the backseat and retrieved the small satchel he'd brought from the cottage.

"What's in that anyway?" she asked.

"It's just Angela's bag of tricks." He opened the satchel. "I added a few of my own."

Her pulse rate tripled as he began pulling out items she couldn't begin to identify. A tiny black box with what looked like six inches of cord hanging from it. Another item that looked like a miniature garage-door opener. An odd-looking pistol that appeared to be made of plastic. "A gun?" she asked.

"Dart gun. Nonlethal. It delivers a potent tranquilizer."

"In case someone shows up?"

"The fire will take care of the officers on duty, keep them busy for a while. But I expect there will be others who remain at the station." His smile looked as lethal as the gun. "Don't want to kill any cops."

Jess pressed her hand to her stomach at the thought of confronting any of the Lighthouse Point cops. She'd never broken the law before, and she didn't like the feeling. Even if it was for a much greater good.

Madrid reached up and unscrewed the dome light again. "Slide behind the wheel."

Even though the night was chilly, sweat broke out on the back of her neck when he got out of the car. Her palms were wet with sweat when she slid across the seat and set her hands on the steering wheel.

"Are you sure you can handle this?" he asked.

She wasn't. Not by a long shot. But it was too late to turn back now. If she wanted Angela's killer to be caught, they were going to have to go through with this. "I'm sure."

He quietly closed the driver's side door and looked around. "I want you to stay here for exactly ten minutes in the alley."

She checked the clock on the dash. "Okay."

"Then I want you to drive over to the new police department building. I'll be waiting." He put the items back into the satchel and hooked it on his belt.

"Once you pick me up, things are going to move fast."

Jess thought things were already moving fast. Too fast, if she wanted to be honest.

"If anything happens...if I get caught...anything, I want you to drive like a bat out of hell back to the coastal highway and head north." Reaching into his pocket, he pulled out a folded piece of paper. "Call this number and someone will pick you up. Tell them everything."

Her hand shook when she reached for the paper. Madrid noticed it, too, and he frowned. He leaned in close, intensity glinting in his eyes when his gaze met hers. Without speaking he kissed her hard on the mouth. Kissing Mike Madrid was like stepping on a live electrical cord. Jess felt her thoughts scramble and her body heat up despite the fear coursing through her. And somehow she knew everything was going to be okay.

Then, as quickly as he had kissed her, he was gone.

Jess sat with both hands on the wheel, her heart pounding, and watched him sprint to the mouth of the alley. His shoes were silent on the asphalt. He moved with the grace of a big dark cat. A predator on the prowl. He became one with the night. And then he was gone, and she was alone.

The minutes seemed to tick by like hours. Two minutes passed. Four. Seven. Around her the area was like a ghost town. Her heart nearly exploded when a vehicle passed by the mouth of the alley, but a glance told her it was only a street sweeper.

One minute to go. Her hand shook uncontrollably when she started the engine. The motor turning over sounded like a gunshot in the dead silence. Looking both ways, she pulled onto the street. She was thirty yards from the construction site when a yellow flicker caught her attention. She stared, her hands gripping the steering wheel so hard her knuckles hurt.

A soft knock on the passenger window nearly sent her out of her skin. All she could think was that Madrid had been caught and she was busted. Both of them would be carted off to jail—or murdered.

But it was only Madrid. She hit the button to unlock the door and he slid smoothly inside.

"Drive," he said as he closed the door. "Nice and easy. Don't speed."

The urge to floor the accelerator was strong, but Jess resisted. She knew it would be the fastest way to draw attention.

"You okay?" he asked.

"I will be when this is done." She glanced in the rearview in time to see the construction site burst into flames.

Chapter Seven

In the course of his career with the MIDNIGHT Agency, Madrid had broken the law too many times to count. Usually the infractions were inconsequential; nobody had been hurt. It had always been for a greater good. Maybe even to save a life. Still, he didn't like what they were doing. He liked even less dragging Jess into it. The problem was he wasn't sure how to keep her out of it.

"Turn here," he said, motioning toward a back street that would take them to the coastal highway.

"I thought we were going to go to the police station."

"We're taking the long way."

His nerves went taut when a police cruiser with its lights blaring suddenly loomed behind them.

"Oh, my God." Jess gaped at the rearview mirror. "Oh, no."

"It's okay. He's going to pass us on his way to the fire."

Still, the relief that swept through him when the car sped past was palpable. He glanced at Jess. She looked calm on the outside, but he could see her hands wrapped like vises around the steering wheel, her eyes flicking to the rearview mirror every couple of seconds.

"You're doing okay," he said.

"I don't feel okay," she replied. "I feel terrified. Like we're doing something wrong. Like someone might get hurt."

"None of those things are going to happen. Just try to stay calm. Everything's going to be all right."

"Famous last words right before we get busted and dragged off to prison."

Another cop car, lights and siren blaring, streaked past.

"Okay," he said, "turn the car around."

Jess shot him an are-you-out-of-your-mind look. "Madrid…"

"We have to move now." He glanced at his watch. "We have twenty minutes max to get into the police station and look around."

A pent-up sigh slid between her lips as she

turned into a church driveway, then pulled back onto the highway.

"And the cops at the station?" she asked.

"That's where our nonlethal weapons come into play."

"I hate to remind you of this unpleasant little detail, but while we might be using nonlethal weapons, the cops aren't."

"We have the element of surprise on our side. I'm a professional."

"I'm a waitress," she blurted out. "I don't know how to do this."

"You'll do fine, Jess." He looked over his shoulder, made sure there was no one following. "Look at you. You're driving like a pro."

She shook her head. "I don't do anything like a pro. The only thing I do well is screw things up."

He risked a look at her, curiosity nipping at him, and he made a mental note to get to the bottom of that statement later. "Maybe you ought to give yourself a little more credit." He motioned left. "Turn here."

They were on a side street that ran parallel to the main drag. The police station was a block ahead. "Park in that lot over there, beneath the tree."

Jess pulled into the lot and cut the engine

and lights. She knew if she took her hands off
the steering wheel they would shake uncontrollably, so she didn't. Madrid's window was
down a few inches and the chorus of crickets
and frogs was in full swing. In the near distance
she could hear sirens. Dead ahead, the police
station was lit up like a football stadium.

"I count four cars."

She jolted at the sound of Madrid's voice and
jerked her gaze to the parking lot beside the
police station. Sure enough, four cars sat
beneath the glow of the streetlight.

"I'm hoping that doesn't mean there are four
cops inside," she said.

"Most cops drive their own car to work, then
switch to their city car. More cars than people
here, I'd say."

Jess wished her heart would slow down. She
felt shaky and scared and she hated it. "How
many inside?"

"At this hour and for a town this size, I'd say
there's a dispatcher and maybe two officers."

Sick with nerves, she pressed her hand to her
stomach. "How are we going to handle that
many people?"

"I have a plan."

"Of course you do."

He grinned, but for the first time Jess thought she saw the sharp edge of nerves beneath the reckless facade. She watched as he dug into the satchel and pulled out a small packet of what looked like ketchup. "Don't tell me you have fries to go with that."

"Just a tall tale." He tore open the packet with his teeth, then proceeded to smear what looked like blood on his temple.

Understanding dawned in an unpleasant rush. When he made eye contact, Jess could have sworn the blood was real. "Not bad."

Madrid said, "I'm going to walk in and tell them I was driving on the coastal highway and someone took a shot at my car. I was nicked in the temple. That ought to distract them long enough for me to get the upper hand."

It was good as far as stories went. A situation the police would surely need to investigate. But there were so many things that could go wrong.

She realized then he hadn't included her in the story. One look at his face and she knew why. He was concerned for her safety. She knew it was silly, but his concern warmed her in a place that hadn't been warmed for a very long time.

"Madrid, you can't do this alone."

"I don't think you're in any shape to—"

"I can do it," she cut in.

"Jess…" He scraped a hand over his face. "You can't. They'll recognize you—they're looking for you."

She shook her head. "They're looking for a woman with a little boy. I have to take the chance, Madrid. For Angela and Nicolas. For me."

He stared at her with such intensity that it was difficult to hold his gaze. Then he nodded and his eyes went back to the police station. "Okay. Same story. You're my wife. All you have to do is help me in. I was driving when some unknown gunman took a potshot at us. Okay?"

There was nothing okay about any of this, but Jess nodded. She wondered if he could see the fear that was surely written all over her face.

When Madrid got out of the car, Jess followed, hating that her legs were weak and shaking. Out of the corner of her eye she saw him smear more of the fake blood on his shirt. She crossed around the front of the car and jolted when he reached for her and applied some of the blood to her hands.

"You sure you can handle this?" he asked.

His hands were warm and strong and incredibly reassuring as they covered hers. "I'm sure."

"Let's go." He looked both ways, then put his arm around her shoulder. "Put your arm around me," he said. "As if you're helping me."

She did. He was large and warm beside her. When he leaned on her she thought she detected a quiver, but he didn't give her time to ponder. "We move fast from here," he said.

They crossed the street at a jog with Madrid leaning heavily against her. Her legs trembled as they ascended the concrete steps that would take them inside. Through double glass doors she saw what was probably the desk sergeant's desk. Beyond, a narrow hall led to several offices. Their doors were open, though only one of the lights was on.

She shoved open one of the double doors and they walked inside, Madrid groaning loudly in a believable performance. She realized he was a much better actor than she was.

"Call for help," he whispered.

Jess closed her eyes, prayed for strength. "Help us!" she called out. "Please, there's been a shooting."

A young cop who didn't look old enough to shave emerged from the lit office. His eyes widened at the sight of him. "What happened?" he asked, rushing toward them.

"Someone shot at us," Jess said in a strangled voice.

Madrid groaned again.

"My h-husband is hurt. We need an ambulance."

The young cop went for his radio. "Where?"

"On the h-highway."

A middle-aged cop wearing an ill-fitting uniform emerged from another office. His mouth opened when he saw them. "What's going on here?"

"Shot out on the highway." The young cop motioned toward a wood bench against the wall. "I'll call an ambulance. Sit him down there. We'll get someone on the scene."

The second cop turned and shouted. "Dispatch! Get on the horn! Shots fired on the coast high—"

Jess didn't even see Madrid go for the tiny plastic pistol he'd tucked into his waistband. But in the next instant it was in his hand.

"What the—"

The young cop didn't have time to finish the sentence. The gun let out a whispered *poink*. The young cop grabbed his throat, staggered to the left. Jess gasped when she saw the dart protruding from his neck. He raised the radio, but Madrid kicked it from the man's hand.

"Hey! You can't—"

Madrid spun, brought up the dart gun. *Poink!* The middle-aged cop jolted when a dart slammed into his shoulder. A curse slid from his mouth as he fumbled for his radio. Madrid fired again, this time striking him in the gut. The cop stumbled, dropped his radio. Madrid moved with the speed and grace of a big cat and kicked the radio away, out of reach.

Jess thought her heart was going to explode. Out of the corner of her eye she saw the young cop fall to his knees, clutching his throat. He made a strangled sound and collapsed. The older cop was already on the ground, inching like a big worm toward the fallen radio. But Madrid was faster and crushed it beneath his boot.

He swung his gaze toward Jess. "We need to clear the rest of the building."

Jess glanced down the hall, but no one had emerged. She looked back to the two men who lay motionless on the floor now.

Madrid sprinted down the hall. When he'd cleared the first two offices, a third young cop darted from a room farther down the hall.

"What the hell—"

Madrid fired twice in quick succession. The cop did an awkward dance as two darts hit home, one in the throat, the other in his stomach. His hands fluttered over the weapon strapped to his side, but before he could reach it his eyes rolled back. His knees buckled. His body hit the floor like a sack of flour.

Three cops down in less than two minutes. Jess couldn't believe they'd gotten this far.

"Find Mummert's office," Madrid said as he dragged the first man into a darkened office, out of sight from the lobby and street.

For an instant Jess was so scared she couldn't move. Then, numbly, she started down the hall. The first office she passed was Dispatch. Inside, she could see a computer monitor and a switch-board-like system. The next office was labeled Norm Mummert, Chief Of Police. "Here," she heard herself say.

With the three unconscious men stowed out of sight, Madrid strode past her into the office and went directly to the desk. "Check the file cabinet."

Jess's entire body shook as she darted to the cabinet. She couldn't stop thinking about the three cops lying unconscious on the floor or the very real possibility that another one would walk through the door and catch them red-handed.

"What are we looking for?" she asked.

"Same kind of thing we were looking for back at Angela's. Anything unusual or suspicious. Photos. Documents. I don't know."

She tugged at a cabinet drawer, only to discover it was locked. "Damn."

Madrid already had the top drawer of the desk open. He stopped what he was doing and reached the file cabinet in two strides. "We don't have time to finesse this."

Jess shouldn't have been surprised when he slid a big black pistol from his waistband. "How many guns are you carrying, anyway?" she muttered.

"Enough to get the job done." He fired a shot directly into the lock. Even though the gun was equipped with a silencer, the single shot seemed thunderous.

The drawer rolled open, its mangled lock smoking like a spent match.

"Go," Madrid said. "We've only got a few minutes."

Jess didn't have to be told twice. As methodically as she could manage, she went through each file, but found nothing even remotely suspicious. The second drawer proved just as useless. By the time she finished with the cabinet, frustration and the ever-present fear of discovery were quickly transforming into panic.

"Nothing," she said.

Madrid finished with the desk. "Maybe there's a file or storage room."

"How long will that tranquilizer last?" she asked.

"Half an hour tops." His gaze met hers. "You doing okay?"

She gave him a smile, but it felt shaky on her face. "I don't know how criminals do this stuff. It's nerve-racking."

"Different wiring." He reached out, touched her shoulder gently. "Let's look for the file room."

His touch reassured her the way nothing else could have at that moment. Then he was moving past her and into the hall. She followed closely behind him. Looking ahead, she saw a room labeled Records. "There," she said.

"Bingo."

His hand was resting on the gun tucked into the waistband of his jeans as he entered the room and flipped on the light. It was the size of a walk-in closet, but from floor to ceiling the room was filled with some type of paper storage system, from file cabinets to cardboard record storage boxes to steel shelving units.

"I don't think we can get through all this in five minutes," she said.

"We'll go through what we can. Leave the rest." He looked around. "I'll take the file cabinet." He tugged at the first drawer. When it didn't open, he pulled the gun and shot the lock. The drawer rolled open. Madrid pulled out the first file and began to page through it at the pace of a speed-reader.

Jess turned and, uncertain where to start, crossed to the nearest shelf and pulled down a box. The box itself was marked Parking Tickets. She figured if someone was trying to hide something, he'd label the goods with an innocent, ordinary title. Quickly she paged through each folder, finding nothing.

Urgency hammered at her as she went to the next box. Seconds ticked into minutes as they worked. Midway through the box, she glanced at her watch and was alarmed to realize they'd been inside for fifteen minutes.

Hurry.

Closing her eyes against a rise of panic, she slid the box onto the shelf and went to the next. This one was labeled Arrest Reports from several years earlier. Someone was behind on their filing. Discouraged and scared, certain she wasn't going to find anything, Jess began paging through the files.

She was no cop, but she realized almost immediately these were not arrest reports. They looked like some type of profile. Psychological. Physical. A dossier of sorts on young, foreign-born women complete with photographs, background information and health reports.

"I think I found something," she said.

Madrid left the file he was frantically digging through and crossed to her. He looked down at the dossier in her hand. "I'll be damned." He went to the next document.

"What is it?"

Madrid made a sound low in his throat. "Looks like some sort of blueprint."

"Blueprint of what?"

"Hard to tell from this." He went to the next page. "Looks like a container. Like some sort of ship modification."

"A container ship?"

He set his finger against the drawing. "There's been a compartment built into the aft side. Looks like some sort of crude living quarters."

Jess stared at the architectural drawing, her heart pounding. The tiny type illustrated a small bunk area, a sink and toilet facility.

"My God," she murmured. "A floating prison."

His eyes were dark with knowledge when they met hers. "I think we just hit pay dirt."

"Let's hope we fare better than these passengers."

Her words were punctuated by the sound of the outer door opening.

Chapter Eight

Madrid heard the door close as if it were a gunshot. Adrenaline stung his gut. Automatically his hand went to the dart gun. Only, he didn't have any more darts. The last thing he wanted to do was shoot a cop—even if there was a good possibility said cop was corrupt. But he pulled the revolver from his waistband anyway.

Human smuggling was a lucrative trade. But it was also a violent, immoral one. He knew whoever was responsible wouldn't leave any witnesses. Not alive, anyway.

In a fraction of a second his mind ran through a dozen scenarios, none of them good. The best he could hope for was to get out alive.

"Go out the window." He strode briskly to the window above a lateral file cabinet, realizing immediately there was no way he could fit through it. But Jess could.

Twisting the lock, he flung it open as wide as it would go. "Run to the car."

"I'm not leaving without you."

He continued as if he hadn't heard her. "If I'm not there in three minutes, I want you to drive like a bat out of hell to the coast highway. Don't stop until you're out of the state."

"Madrid—"

"If you get caught, tell them I took you hostage. That I was going to kill you."

"But—"

"There's no time to argue!"

Jess went pale right before his eyes and for an instant he got the uneasy feeling she was going to faint. Damn. Damn. *Damn!*

Glancing over his shoulder at the door, half expecting to see a cop with a big gun and an itchy trigger finger, he muscled her to the window. "Go, damn it. I can take care of myself," he whispered, hoping to get her moving before she had too much time to think about it. The last thing he needed was for her to worry about him.

She took one last look at him, shook her head and went through the open window. Hoping she stuck to the plan, relieved that he didn't have to worry about her, Madrid darted to the door and peered around the doorjamb.

The cop was standing at the sergeant's desk, looking around suspiciously. "Hey, Dex! Where the hell are you?" He put his hands on his hips and started toward the hall. "Must be a damn full moon. All hell's breaking loose out there."

Madrid spun, darted to the storage box and grabbed what documents he could, then stuffed them into the waistband of his slacks. Every nerve in his body went taut when he heard a shout in the hall. Undoubtedly the cop had discovered his buddies.

Cursing beneath his breath, knowing he'd run out of time and options, Madrid looked around wildly. But there was no escape.

Footsteps sounded outside the door, followed by the steel click of a hammer being pulled back.

He pulled his fake FBI identification from his slacks. "FBI!" he shouted. "SAC Magill! Don't shoot!"

The burly officer appeared in the doorway. He glared at Madrid. His gaze flashed to the ID Madrid held in his hand, but he didn't lower the gun.

"Who the hell are you?"

"Mike Magill, Special Agent in Charge. FBI." Remembering the fake blood, Madrid looked down at his shirt. "I heard shots. Someone jumped me from behind."

"What are you doing here?"

"I had a meeting with Norm Mummert."

The cop's gun hand relaxed marginally. He looked over his shoulder, toward his fallen comrades. "What happened?"

"Two men, well armed. I ducked into this office." He winced dramatically. "I'm hit."

The cop lowered his gun and reached for his radio. "This is Two Adam Four. I got a—"

Madrid lunged, kicked the gun from the other man's hand. The cop's eyes went wide. He reeled backward, screamed into the radio, "Code eight!"

Madrid knew enough about cop jargon to know that was the code for an officer calling an emergency. He knew that in seconds the place would be crawling with cops out to protect one of their own. The kind of situation that called for deadly force. Hell.

Madrid spun, kicked the radio from the man's hand. Vaguely he was aware of it clattering to the floor. The cop's eyes flicked to the fallen gun six feet away.

"Don't do it," Madrid growled.

The cop dived for the weapon.

Cursing, Madrid went for the cop, but he wasn't fast enough to keep him from grabbing the gun. They rolled in a tangle of arms and legs and fists. What the officer lacked in the art of self-defense, he made up for in size.

In the struggle Madrid caught a glimpse of the blue steel muzzle, then a white-knuckled fist. The ensuing blast made his ears ring, followed by plaster raining down from the ceiling where the bullet had blown through.

Madrid tried to wrestle the gun away, but the cop was too big. He kneed Madrid, loosening his grip for just a second, and rolled away. In one swift motion the gun came up and the muzzle exploded. The next thing Madrid knew his arm was on fire. It felt as if someone had sneaked up behind him and branded him with a hot poker.

More pain followed in a sickening rush. But it made him mad. Furious, in fact. He used the resulting adrenaline to put the other man on his back.

"You just had to cross that line, didn't you?"

Grabbing the other man's wrist, Madrid slammed it against the floor. Once. Twice. "Drop it!" he shouted.

The cop's hand opened and the gun clattered

away. Clamping his hand around the cop's throat, Madrid tugged the handcuffs from his belt with his free hand. He closed one cuff around the man's wrist, the other around the shelving unit brace.

"That ought to hold you for a while." Dizziness assailed him when he rose. Surprised, he leaned against the file cabinet. He glanced down at his arm, saw blood coming through his jacket and cursed.

The cop yanked at the cuff. "You won't get away, you son of a bitch!"

"I already have," Madrid said, and walked out the door.

JESS HAD NEVER BEEN GOOD at waiting. But if waiting was torture, then sitting in the car, waiting to see if Madrid would make it out of that building alive, was nothing short of hell.

She couldn't see the front of the building from where she was parked, but with her window down she'd heard the shots. And the thought of all the things that could be going on inside made her sick.

A glance at the clock on the dash told her six minutes had passed, but it felt as if she'd been waiting an eternity. Was Madrid in trouble? Had the cop shot him? Or had the agent with the dark eyes been forced to do the unthinkable and shoot a cop?

"Come on, Madrid." Her voice sounded strained in the silence of the car. She tried drumming her fingers on the steering wheel, but they were shaking too much. She couldn't take her eyes off the stretch of sidewalk leading to the police station....

A strangled yelp escaped her when she heard a tap on the passenger window. Half expecting to see a cop with a gun, she glanced over to see Madrid standing there, looking inside. Weak with relief, she hit the locks.

"What took you so long?" she hissed as she started the engine.

He slid onto the seat. "Drive."

Jess jammed the car into gear. The tires squealed as she pulled onto the street.

"Easy," Madrid said. "We don't want to draw any attention."

"God forbid someone might think we just burglarized the police department." Jess figured they would be drawing plenty of attention very soon. The wrong kind. "What happened in there?"

Grimacing, he leaned back in the seat and glanced down. Jess looked over from her driving and followed his stare. "Oh, my God." Her heart began to pound as she took in the amount of real blood soaking his shirt. "You've been shot."

"That just about sums it up."

"How bad?"

"Bad enough."

The blood oozed black in the semidarkness. She couldn't stop looking at it.

"Watch where you're going."

She glanced back at the road just in time to keep the wheels from going off the pavement.

"You need to calm down," he said. "Slow down. This'll hold for a little while."

They were on the coast highway now. Jess glanced at the speedometer, inched it back down to sixty. The last thing they needed was to be pulled over. "Did you get the papers and photos?" she asked.

He scowled, shook his head. "I grabbed what I could, but I lost most of it when the cop jumped me."

She gaped at him. "A cop jumped you?"

"Long story."

Jess hoped he had enough of the documents to figure out what the Lighthouse Point PD was into.

"Where are we going?" she asked.

"Just drive." Worry crept into her mind when he leaned against the seat and put his head against the rest.

"Are you going to be all right?"

"I'm always all right." He grinned, but she saw the stress around the edges. He was in pain and bleeding. As far as she knew, the bullet could have broken his arm or perforated a vein.

Using his right hand he eased his cell phone from his pocket. He punched numbers, then put the phone to his ear. "It's me." His voice was low and rough. "I need sanctuary. Code one. Level blackjack."

He listened for a minute, then without speaking closed the phone and shoved it back into his pocket.

"Who was that?" Jess asked.

"Cavalry." He pointed to a gravel lane. "Turn around. Head north."

Jess turned into the lane, then backed out and turned the car around. "Where are we going?"

"Church."

"Back to Father Matthew's church?"

Madrid shook his head. "I've already involved him enough. There's an old mission an hour to the north. A safe house set up by the MIDNIGHT Agency."

"I thought you quit."

He lifted his shoulder as if to shrug, but winced instead. "This is unofficial."

Jess glanced at him. A sheen of sweat covered his face. His mouth was set in a thin, taut line, his eyes dark and glassy with pain. "I hope they have first aid supplies," she said.

"We'll find out when we get there." Closing his eyes, he leaned against the seat.

IN THE SIX YEARS he'd been with the MIDNIGHT Agency Madrid had been forced to function countless times in extremely uncomfortable situations. This time, however, the pain radiating from his shoulder to his fingertips was far worse than mere discomfort.

By the time they pulled into the weed-riddled parking lot of the tiny mission, his tolerance had worn down to a thin veneer. He could feel the pain pulsing through his system with every beat of his heart. He was sweating and irritable and a hell of a lot more shaky than he wanted to admit. He didn't know if the bullet had gone clean through or if he was going to have to talk Jess into digging it out. The thought sent a wave of nausea washing over him.

Even though the abandoned mission was half

a mile from the coast highway, he had Jess park beneath the canopies of a grove of cedar elms so the car couldn't be spotted via police helicopter.

"You look terrible," she said as she shut down the engine.

"All the women tell me that." He tried to smile, but didn't think he managed. He was too worried about whether or not he could make it inside on his own power.

The clock on the dash read 3:00 a.m. It was too dark for him to assess the wound, but he could feel the blood beginning to clot, causing his shirt to stick to his skin. Damn, he hoped it wasn't as bad as it felt.

Grimacing, he reached for the satchel and removed a tiny flashlight. "Let's go inside and see what accommodations the MIDNIGHT Agency has provided." He shoved open the door.

"Maybe you ought to let me help you."

"I'm fine," he said, and got out of the car.

Madrid wasn't exactly sure what happened next. One moment he was walking toward the single-level stucco mission. The next he was on his knees, clutching his arm, trying not to throw up.

"Madrid!" Jess rushed to him and knelt at his side.

Vaguely he was aware of her putting her arm

around him. She was warm and soft against him. She smelled like sandalwood, only sweeter. Through the pain he was aware of her breast brushing his shoulder. It had been a long time since he'd been this close to a woman, and the feeling was damn nice.

Slowly the nausea subsided and the dizziness leveled off.

"How bad is the wound?" she asked after a moment.

"Anytime a piece of lead penetrates skin, it's bad," he growled.

"Can you make it inside?"

"Unless you're a hell of a lot stronger than you look, I don't think I have a choice."

She usurped the flashlight. "I can handle the light."

A groan escaped him as he heaved himself from the ground. Jess put her arm around his waist and draped his uninjured arm around her shoulders. He didn't let himself think about the pain or dizziness as they wobbled toward the mission.

"We go in the back," Madrid said between gritted teeth.

"Okay." Jess shoved open a rusty wrought-iron gate and set the beam on a gravel path that led to a courtyard. Madrid barely noticed the defunct fountain that had once been grand. At the rear of the mission she tried the door, found it locked.

"What now?" she asked.

He looked around, spotted a nice-size stone that had once been part of a flower bed, then realized he wasn't going to be able to bend over to pick it up. "We break the glass." He motioned toward the rock.

Jess scooped it up.

Madrid took it from her and in a single smooth motion shattered the pane nearest the lock. Shoving his hand inside, he fumbled around for the bolt, flipped it and pushed open the door. The odors of mildew and old wood met his nose as he stepped inside.

"Home sweet home," he said.

"Please tell me there's electricity."

"That would be way too convenient." He handed her the flashlight. "We'll be lucky if there are candles."

They had entered through what had once been a kitchen. A wooden table with peeling paint and four mismatched chairs stood in the center of the room. Madrid pulled out a chair and collapsed into it. Vaguely he was aware of

Jess moving around, the beam bobbing off to his left.

"I found supplies!"

He looked up to see Jess approach, her arms full, and smiling as if she'd just won the lotto. Madrid stared at her, taken aback by the hard tug of attraction. Damn, he wished she wasn't so pretty. He'd always been attracted to pretty things.

She set the supplies on the table. Digging into a box, she removed two candles, lit them, and yellow light illuminated the room.

"Looks like there's food in here, too," she said.

"What about a first aid kit?" Every MID-NIGHT Agency safe house would include something for emergencies.

"Check." She took the red-and-white kit from the box. "There's also a flashlight, bottled water." She went still. "A pistol."

"Must be our lucky day." But he hoped they weren't going to need it.

Her gaze met his. "Will we be safe here?"

"For tonight. The Agency is meticulous about choosing its safe houses. You can bet this place isn't on the map or tax roll."

"What exactly does this agency do?"

"The things no other agency will touch."

She thought about that for a moment. "Serious stuff."

"Yeah." Because it was best she didn't know any more than she already did, Madrid changed the subject. "I need to take a look at this wound. Get it cleaned up." Gingerly he worked the jacket off his shoulders.

"Maybe we ought to get you to a hospital."

"No can do."

"Madrid—"

"If you're not up to it, I can do it myself."

"I don't think you're in any condition to do much of anything."

As much as he hated to admit it, she was right. "Look, if it's bad we'll do what we need to do. For now, let's get it cleaned up and see what we're dealing with."

A sigh of resignation shuddered out of her. "I'm a waitress. I don't know anything about treating bullet wounds."

He managed a smile. "Yeah, but you're a quick study."

Chapter Nine

Up until two days ago Jess hadn't so much as seen a bullet wound, let alone get shot at, sustain one herself or administer first aid. Angela's murder had changed everything. She wasn't squeamish; she'd treated her own bullet wound just days before. But treating someone else's was a completely different endeavor.

Next to her, Madrid draped his jacket over the back of his chair and proceeded to remove his shirt. In the yellow glow of the candles she saw wide shoulders and a broad chest covered with a thatch of dark hair. She swallowed hard as his washboard abs came into view. He was muscular, but not overdeveloped. She knew it was silly considering the circumstances, but she'd never seen such a magnificent male body.

She didn't know if it was the utter maleness of him or the thought of treating a potentially serious wound, but she began to tremble. She could feel the hot zing of nerves running through her body, making her knees weak, her fingers twitchy. Not a good reaction considering what she was about to do.

She picked up the first aid kit, opened it, closed it, then repeated the action. When she ran out of things to do, she turned back to Madrid.

He'd settled into the chair. Leaning against the back, he might have look relaxed, if he hadn't been cradling his left arm. Jess didn't want to do this. She didn't want to treat him or look at the wound. But with nowhere to turn, nowhere to go, no one to call for help, she knew she didn't have a choice.

Pulling up a chair beside his, she sat and peered at the wound. The blood looked black in the candlelight. The surrounding skin was beginning to swell, but there was too much blood for her to assess the wound fully.

"There's probably alcohol in the kit."

She started at the sound of Madrid's voice. She glanced at him to find his eyes already on her. Gathering the jagged remains of her composure, she reached for the kit. Sure enough, a dozen or so alcohol packets were nestled inside next to a roll of sterile gauze and a suture kit.

"Pretty extensive first aid kit," she muttered.

"Practical for our line of work."

She tried not to think about that as she opened a package and carefully disinfected her hands.

"Your hands are shaking."

"Yeah, well, bullet wounds make me nervous."

With his good arm he reached out and touched her. "We're safe for now," he said, misinterpreting the cause of her shakiness. "We've got a few hours. Try to relax."

"That's only part of it, Madrid." She motioned toward the wound. "It looks bad, and I'm not very good at this. I don't want to hurt you."

"I'll let you know when it hurts."

"If you don't pass out first."

"I'm not going to pass out, okay?"

"Like you have any control."

Grimacing, he turned his arm so he could get a better look. "Did the bullet go in and out?"

She'd been putting off looking at it, but she had no choice. "There's some swelling. I'll need to wipe off some of this blood."

He handed her an alcohol packet. "Do what you can. Don't worry about hurting me. I'm okay."

But would he be okay once she started probing the wound? Taking the swab, she took a deep breath and dabbed at the bloody skin.

Next to her, Madrid sat stone still, watching. "No exit wound," he said. "See if you can feel the bullet."

Jess palpated the area as gently as she could, jerking her hand away when he hissed out a curse. "Sorry."

"Dig it out."

She looked up to find his gaze already on hers. In the dim light she could see the sheen of sweat on his forehead. The grim line of his mouth. "Madrid…"

"Infection will set in if you don't." He paused. "Come on, Jess. It's not deep."

Her own wound hadn't been nearly as bad. It had bled a lot, but the bullet had grazed her. Still, hers had gotten infected and could have become extremely serious if Madrid hadn't given her antibiotics.

"Madrid, you need to see a doctor."

"I need to be able to function," he snapped. "Now, either you're going to dig it out or I am."

Jess could only imagine the pain it would cause him for her to dig the bullet out. But like a lot of other things that were happening at the moment, all choice had been taken from her.

Reaching into the kit, she found a package of

ibuprofen and handed it to him. "You're going to need these."

"Kind of like trying to put out a fire with a squirt gun." He swallowed the pills dry, then gingerly set his arm on the table. "Just think of it as a big splinter."

"That's not helping."

Using the flashlight, Jess located the sterile tools, a needle, tweezers and scissors. Her heart was beating hard and fast when she turned back to him. But not all the tension inside her was due to the wound. Part of it, she knew, was because he wasn't wearing a shirt. Because he was too close. Too *male*. And in all of her twenty-eight years, she'd never seen a chest like Mike Madrid's.

She moved the candle closer, shifted his arm for a better angle. Sure enough, she could see the lump of the bullet beneath the skin. Picking up the tweezers, she touched the wound. When he didn't wince, she slid the sterile tip into the wound. She could feel his muscles tightening beneath her hand, but he didn't make a sound.

"Here goes." She probed deeper. A sigh hissed between his lips, but she didn't stop. A fraction of an inch and the tweezers made contact with the bullet. If only she could grasp it.

A groan escaped him when she let the tweezers open. Fresh blood trickled down his arm when she clamped down on the bullet. "My God…"

"Let it bleed." He ground out the words. "Get the bullet. Do it. Now."

Though the mission was chilly, sweat beaded on her forehead as she pulled on the tweezers. An instant of resistance and the bloody piece of lead was free.

"I got it."

Madrid shifted, and Jess got the impression of him holding his breath. Quickly she tore open another alcohol pad and dabbed at the blood. "I don't think you need stitches."

"Good, because I'd hate for you to have to pick me up off the floor."

She looked at him. Alarm shot through her when she realized he'd gone white. "I'm sorry I hurt you."

"It's okay." He glanced at the wound, closed his eyes briefly. "You did well."

"Let me just get it cleaned up." She opened another swab. "Alcohol is going to burn."

"Better than dying of infection."

"Or evidently doing the smart thing and going to the hospital."

He didn't so much as flinch when she

swabbed the gash. She felt one of them shaking, but for the life of her she couldn't tell if it was him or her.

She spent a few minutes bandaging the wound. When she finished, she rose on unsteady legs. Madrid leaned forward in the chair and put his head on the table as if the ordeal had drained him of all strength.

"You need to promise me one thing," she said as she began putting items back into the first aid kit.

But when she turned back to Madrid, he was out cold.

MADRID WOKE TO DAYLIGHT. For a moment he was mildly surprised he'd made it through the night. Pain throbbed in his left arm. Above him, dust motes danced on the air where sunlight streamed in through a window.

He sat up, cursing when pain streaked up his arm. He lay back down and for an uncomfortable moment he wasn't quite sure where he was. Then the memory of everything that had happened the night before rushed over him in a flood. He and Jess breaking into Angela's house and the police station. The sound of gunshots. Running through the night. The emergency call to the agency. Jess digging a bullet out of his arm.

The knowledge that they were still in danger sent him back upright, gingerly this time. He was lying on an old sofa, tangled in a single blanket. On the floor next to him, Jess lay on her side, shivering in her sleep. She had no blanket. No pillow. She'd given both to him.

"Damn," he whispered, and something went soft in his chest.

Even with her hair mussed, her face devoid of makeup, her beauty took him aback. She'd wrapped herself with her jacket, but it didn't cover her completely and he was keenly aware of curvy hips and the soft swell of her breasts. That she'd sacrificed her own comfort for his touched him in a place that hadn't been touched in a very long time.

A powerful wave of affection washed over him, followed by a hard jab of sexual attraction. He didn't want to admit either. He knew all too well the kinds of things that happened to the people he cared about. For some reason God had seen to it that the people he loved never survived long enough for him to tell them how he felt. First his parents. Then his wife and child. Angela. Was this woman next on fate's hit list?

"Morning."

He started at the unexpected greeting and jerked his gaze back to her. She tugged the jacket up to her chin and stretched like a cat. "How are you feeling?"

Considering the way those jeans were stretching taut over her hips, he didn't think the truth was appropriate, so he settled on a half-truth. "A little rough around the edges."

He watched her rise. Every male hormone in his body jumped to attention when she strode to the hall, where he assumed there was a bathroom. He lay there a moment, ordering his libido to settle down. An instant later the sound of running water reached him and he realized the place had an operable shower.

Silently thanking the MIDNIGHT Agency, he struggled to his feet. The pain in his arm snarled as he made his way to the kitchen and looked in the cabinets for coffee. Sure enough, two packages of instant coffee gleamed up at him like gold.

By the time he'd made two cups, Jess had come out of the shower. Her hair was curly and wet, her cheeks pink. Madrid shoved one of the cups at her, trying not to notice the way that old sweatshirt clung to curves he had absolutely no business noticing.

"Where on earth did you find coffee?" she asked.

"Right next to the protein bars and the camp stove." Looking into her eyes, he found it easy to smile, even through the pain and the knowledge that he needed a shower.

"Chocolate?"

"Of course." He handed her one of the bars. Something warm and uncomfortable fluttered inside him when she smiled back. Damn, she had the prettiest smile he'd ever seen.

Realizing he was doing the one thing he shouldn't, he crossed to the counter where he'd left the photos he'd confiscated the night before from the Lighthouse Point PD.

"I thought we'd go through this and see if we can figure out what the hell's going on." Easing himself into a chair, he spread six photos on the table. "I wish I'd been able to grab more."

"Kind of hard when someone's shooting at you." Jess took the chair next to his and looked at the photos. "What are we looking for?"

"Something that might give us a clue as to where these women are being held." He wished for the magnification/high resolution software available at MIDNIGHT headquarters, but knew he would have to rely on his naked eye this time around. "Logo on a shirt. License plate number. Street sign." He sighed. "As far as we know, this may not even be taking place in the United States."

"But you think these women are ultimately ending up here, right?"

He grimaced. "Yeah."

They studied the scant evidence spread out before them. After a moment Jess leaned forward and put her finger against one of the photos. "What about this?"

The photo depicted two frightened-looking women with their hands bound behind their backs. Madrid hadn't been able to discern where they were standing, because the background was blurred. But in the far right-hand corner there was a tiny round porthole. Through the porthole several letters were visible. "*X-A-N-A,*" he recited.

"What do they mean?"

His heart beat faster. "I can't believe I didn't notice this sooner."

"What is it?"

"Looks like part of the name of a ship." He glanced over at her.

"The ship where these women are being held?" she asked excitedly.

Tearing his gaze away from her, he focused on the photo. "What we're seeing is the bow of another ship through the window."

"How is that going to help us?"

"If I can figure out the full name of the ship, we might be able to find the port where it's docked."

"Seems like a big undertaking, considering our resources."

"It's a long shot, but we might get lucky."

The one thing Madrid was sure of was that to do either of those things, he would need to contact the MIDNIGHT Agency. It was something he hadn't wanted to do again, but he knew he didn't have a choice. He had a sinking suspicion Angela had been onto something a lot bigger than anyone had anticipated.

"Let's see if Santa left us a cell phone that can't be traced."

Jess's brows went together. "Santa?"

Given that the place was a MIDNIGHT Agency safe house, there was a good chance an untraceable cell phone had been supplied. Madrid began going through the box of supplies Jess had found the night before. Sure enough, buried beneath the bottled water and batteries was a tiny cell phone.

Quickly he punched in the number from memory and waited. Jake Vanderpol answered on the second ring. "Don't tell me," he began without preamble. "You need a favor."

Madrid couldn't help it; he smiled. "I need a miracle, but a favor will do."

"Cutter called a meeting yesterday, told us not to help you."

"I was wondering why you didn't call me back."

"Not only has Cutter been a pain about this, but information has been tough to come by. I'm still working on a few things."

But uncertainty fluttered uncomfortably inside Madrid. "I wouldn't put you on the spot like this if it wasn't important."

A beat of silence, then Jake sighed. "Madrid, you are going to owe me big-time."

"I need to know the name of the port where a cargo or container ship is docked."

"U.S.?"

"Probably."

"What's the hull number?"

"All I have is a partial name. *X-A-N-A.*"

"Well, that ought to make it easy," Jake said dryly.

"How soon can you get it for me?"

"Give me an hour."

"I'll be waiting," Madrid said. He gave him the cell phone number and snapped the phone closed.

JESS LISTENED to the clang of the old water pipes and tried hard not to envision Mike Madrid naked beneath the spray. As far as she was concerned, she'd seen far too much of him the night before when she'd treated his gunshot wound. She told herself she had no desire to see more. But Jess had always been truthful with herself; she wanted to see more of him. A lot more. She just didn't like the edgy need that engulfed her every time she laid eyes on him. She'd screwed up enough relationships in her lifetime to know anything more than the tentative friendship they'd forged would never work.

She busied herself studying the photos as he showered. She wanted to call Father Matthew to check on Nicolas, but wouldn't do that without clearing it with Madrid first.

"Jess."

At the sound of Madrid's voice she spun around to see him standing in the kitchen doorway. His hair was damp and curling at the ends. Even though he'd had to put on the same shirt and jacket he looked...sexy.

"Is everything all right?" he asked.

"I was just thinking about Nicolas. I want to call him. Is it safe?"

"As long as we keep it short." Unclipping the cell phone from his belt, he punched numbers, then put the phone to his ear. "It's me. Everything okay?" His eyes met Jess's. "Good. I have someone here who wants to talk to you."

He passed the phone to her. He smelled of soap and man, and a string of tension wound through her at his closeness.

"Father Matthew?"

"Hello, Jessica. How are you?"

"I'm okay. How's Nicolas?"

"He's doing fine. One of the sisters has been spending quite a bit of time with him." He chuckled. "The boy has a healthy appetite."

She smiled. A boy's appetite was such a normal, wonderful thing. She wished she could speak to Nicolas, but didn't think he would talk on the phone.

"I can't quite make out the words, but I think he's trying to say something."

In the background she could hear Nicolas. "Mah-mah."

Remembering, Jess closed her eyes. "We think he's asking for his mother. For Angela."

The priest made a sound of sympathy. "Poor child."

"Father Matthew, we think he saw what happened to her."

"What a terrible thing for a child to see. I'll do everything I can to give him comfort."

"Thank you for keeping him for us."

"My pleasure. Be safe."

Jess felt better after talking to Father Matthew. At least Nicolas was safe and in good hands. Now, if she and Madrid could find the people responsible for murdering his mother, all of them could get on with their lives. Maybe even find some closure.

Madrid sat at the table, going through the scant evidence they'd managed to smuggle out of the police headquarters the night before. He looked up when she handed him the phone.

"Everything okay?" he asked.

She nodded. "Your brother is a lifesaver."

"He's saved my ass on a couple of occasions."

The thought made her smile. The contrast between the two men was stark. Though their physical characteristics were similar, their personalities and lifestyles couldn't have been more at odds. "You're lucky to have him."

He grinned. "He doesn't think so sometimes."

She glanced down at the photos spread out on the table. "Did you find anything else?"

"Just the name of the ship. But I think we're onto something big, Jess. Something dangerous someone doesn't want exposed."

"Who?"

"Lighthouse Point PD. We know they're involved, but we don't know who." He grimaced. "They're not the main players."

"How do we find out who the main players are?"

He looked at her and frowned. "First of all, there is no 'we.'"

She frowned back. "I'm involved in this whether you like it or not."

"What I'd like," he said, "is for you to go back to the church and stay with Father Matthew."

It would have been easy to say yes. She was frightened. In the past two days she'd dodged more bullets than most people did in a lifetime. She was worried about Nicolas. Not only was he alone after having so recently lost his mother, but she worried about his safety, too. Nicolas, after all, might have witnessed the murder.

Then Jess remembered Angela's last request— to keep her son safe—and she knew there was no way she could walk away. She couldn't bury her head in the sand and hope everything turned out okay. She'd done that too many times in her life and only made things worse.

"I want to finish this," she said.

He scowled at her. "Things could have turned out a lot worse than they did last night."

"I'm well aware of the dangers."

"You have no idea what we've walked into or what these people are capable of."

She glanced down to where the bullet had grazed her arm. "I think I do."

"Look, Jess, it's admirable that you want to see Angela's killers brought to justice. It's courageous of you to want to be part of it. I can respect that. But you have to be smart about this. The bottom line is you're not trained to deal with any of this."

"Don't even consider trying to talk me out of seeing this through."

"I don't want to see you hurt."

"I've already been hurt." She crossed to him, came within a fraction of an inch of touching him, but pulled back at the last minute. "Lots of people have been hurt. Angela. Nicolas." She motioned toward the table where the photos were spread out like some cheap magazine spread. "The young women in those photos. How can you expect me to walk away?"

"Because you're smart. Because you know I'll handle it."

"You're forgetting one thing, Madrid."

He lifted a brow.

"I made a promise to Angela."

"She wouldn't have wanted you to risk your own life to keep it. Damn it, she asked you to look after her son, not get yourself killed."

"Madrid, these people are not going to stop until he's dead if Nicolas witnessed Angela's murder."

Her own words made her cringe. To think of the innocent little boy being hurt—or worse—made her feel sick inside. But Jess knew this was not the time to mince words. Whatever was going on at the Lighthouse Point PD had to be exposed and stopped.

"I'm going to see this through," she said. "It's up to you whether I finish it with you or without you."

Chapter Ten

Madrid hated waiting, though in the course of
his career he'd been forced to do plenty of it.
Nor did he like staying in one place too long,
especially when some very powerful people
would pay a lot of money to see both him and
Jess dead. And then there was the matter of his
burgeoning feelings for Jess.

The woman was a study in contradictions.
Beautiful and headstrong and vulnerable rolled
into one very intriguing package. Madrid knew
better than to think of her in any terms other
than a witness to a crime he needed to solve.

But he did.

He was attracted to her in a way he'd never
been attracted to another woman in his life. The
chemistry between them was quite simply
something he'd never before experienced—and

he'd had plenty of experience when it came to matters of the flesh.

Pacing the kitchen, he glanced at his watch for the dozenth time, wondering when Vanderpol was going to call. If he was going to call, a little voice chimed in.

Cutter called a meeting yesterday, told us not to help you...

Jake's words rang uncomfortably in his ears. Madrid had figured Cutter wouldn't be happy about his using the MIDNIGHT Agency's resources. But the way Madrid saw it, if he wanted to get to the bottom of Angela's murder, he didn't have a choice.

"You're going to wear a hole in the floor if you keep up that pacing."

Madrid glanced up to see Jess in the kitchen, leaning against the counter, watching him. Attraction tugged hard and low in his gut. It annoyed him. Made him want to do things he knew would only cause them problems later. He figured he had enough problems at the moment without piling on any more.

"It's been a few hours," he growled. "Why the hell hasn't he called?"

She crossed to him, gave him an earnest look that made him think about kissing her. "Maybe he's waiting for a call back, too. Maybe he's still gathering information. Maybe he ran into problems and can't get the information you need."

"Yeah, well, I'm sick of all these damn maybes." Frustrated, he turned away and walked over to the counter.

Dread mixed with anticipation roiled inside him when he heard Jess follow. "If your arm is hurting, there are a few more ibuprofen in the first aid kit."

Madrid gave a curt nod, but he didn't look at her. The pain in his arm was only a small part of what was eating at him. The truth of the matter was he didn't like being cooped up with a woman who turned him into a walking hard-on. A woman he could never have because every person he'd ever cared for had met an untimely death. He didn't want that to happen to Jess.

So why is she here with you now, hotshot?

Because I'm too damn weak to send her away.

"Here."

He actually started at the sound of her voice. He swung around to see her holding two tablets and a bottle of water. "This will help."

Judging by the jump of his pulse, he didn't think so. "Thanks."

He downed the tablets and was halfway

through the water when his cell phone trilled. His gaze went to Jess. She looked back at him, her eyes wide. She crossed her fingers and held them up for him to see.

Madrid unsnapped the cell, saw Vanderpol's name flicker in the window. "What do you have for me?"

"The only container ship I could find with a name even close to the partial you gave me is the *Xanadu Rose*."

"Where?"

"Port of Eureka. Humboldt Bay. California."

"That's not far from here."

"According to shipping records, the ship is docked there right now."

If the records were reliable, Madrid thought.

"Is this something you're going to need backup on?" Jake asked.

"As soon as I find the right vessel, I'll call."

"Don't do anything I wouldn't."

Knowing Jake Vanderpol would do just about anything for his fellow agents, Madrid grinned. "Wouldn't dream of it," he said, and hit the end button.

Jess was already gathering the photos and first aid kit. "Where?" she asked.

"Port of Eureka. Humboldt Bay."

"I know where it is." Her brows went together. "It's an hour from here. By the time we get there it'll be dark."

"Best time of the day for what we have to do."

"If you don't mind the rats."

Madrid picked up the gun, shoved it into his waistband. "Honey, the rats are the least of our worries."

LIGHTNING FLICKERED to the west as Madrid drove slowly past the massive chain-link gates that opened to the shipyard. Intermittent rain spattered against the dirty asphalt. The wind had picked up, sending the surrounding trees into a frantic dance. Jess couldn't think of a worse night for an illegal foray into a shipyard.

A guardhouse stood left of the gate. The bright lights inside revealed two uniformed and armed port police officers.

"I guess that rules out making entry the old-fashioned way," Madrid growled as he sped past.

"So how do we get in?" Jess asked.

"We make our own gate."

"I'm not sure I like the sound of that."

"Getting in is the easy part." He looked away from his driving and made eye contact. "Getting out in one piece is going to iffy."

She liked the sound of that even less.

They had stopped at a discount store and purchased several items before making the drive to Eureka. Bolt cutters. Gloves. Flashlight. Forty feet of rope. A small marine anchor. Disposable camera. A canvas duffel in which to carry everything. Though they were relatively well equipped for the task at hand, Jess thought it was going to take nothing less than a miracle to pull it off.

Madrid parked the car on a muddy road used by a logging company on the north side of the shipyard. The boughs of tall evergreens cloaked them in darkness. On the forest floor, wisps of fog rose like ghostly fingers.

"You up to a walk?"

She glanced over at Madrid. His eyes were sharp and direct in the semidarkness. "I'm up to it," she said a little breathlessly.

"Let's roll."

Quickly he gathered the items they would need, put them in the duffel and they left the car at a jog. Thunder rumbled as they moved silently through the trees. The wet ground squished beneath Jess's sneakers. The wind whispered through the trees. Ahead, Madrid moved with the utter silence of a predator on the prowl.

The forest opened to a grassy plain where a twelve-foot chain-link fence rose out of the ground like a sentinel. Three strands of barbed wire capped the top. Madrid and Jess stopped, and for an instant, the only sounds came from their labored breathing.

He turned to her. "Are you sure you want to do this?"

She thought of Angela and Nicolas and nodded. "I don't want to turn back."

He grimaced. "Okay."

Opening the duffel, Madrid removed the bolt cutters and went to work on the fence. After a dozen snips he'd made a hole big enough for them to pass through. Jess started to duck through it, but he stopped her with a hand on her shoulder. He was so close she could feel the heat coming off his body. For several interminable seconds his dark eyes searched hers.

Jess knew what would happen next, but she was helpless to stop it. It was like standing in the middle of a superhighway, waiting to be mowed down by a speeding eighteen-wheeler.

But when he lowered his mouth to hers, she could think of nothing except the feel of his lips against hers. The kiss was raw and primal and powerful enough to curl her toes and make

the world around her spin like a top. Adrenaline
and desire clashed, like steel dragged across
rock at a high rate of speed, shooting sparks
high into the air.

Jess knew it was crazy, considering where
they were and what they were about to do, but
she kissed him back. She reveled in the feel of
his mouth against hers. The tight grip of his
hands on her shoulders. The tremor she felt run
through his body. She wanted to reach for him,
pull him closer, but as quickly as his mouth had
assailed hers, he pulled back.

Jess blinked, shocked as much by the kiss as
her response to it. "What was that for?"

"Luck."

"If that was a quick peck for luck I'm
almost afraid what will happen when we're
not in a hurry."

For an instant he looked as shocked as she felt.
Then his mouth slowly curved. "It'll be good."

Taking her hand, he ducked through the
opening. Jess followed, her mind reeling, her
body vibrating with the aftershocks of the kiss.
She knew it was silly to be thinking about
something as inconsequential as a kiss when
they were about to risk their lives. But the
truth of the matter was, there was nothing in-

consequential about the way Madrid had
kissed her.

There would be consequences.

He took her past a massive fuel storage tank
and a low, windowless steel building. Two
hundred yards to her left were the lights of the
guardhouse. Dead ahead, a cargo ship stood silhouetted against the night sky, its radar mast
and wheelhouse jutting from an ocean of containers like a mountain of steel.

The hiss of tires against asphalt sent her heart
into her throat. Headlights slashed through the
darkness to her left. The next thing she knew
she was being pulled toward a dozen or so fifty-gallon steel drums stacked haphazardly
against a small building.

"Get down."

Madrid's voice registered at about the same
time a firm hand pressed her head down.

Jess ducked. Her pulse raced wildly as she
peered between two drums. An SUV with some
type of logo painted on the door idled slowly
past. A spotlight mounted near the mirror on the
driver's side shone on the buildings as the SUV
passed. Inside the vehicle, she saw the silhouettes of at least two people.

"Who are they?" she whispered.

"Port police."

"Ironic that we have to dodge the good guys."

"Just because they're wearing the uniform doesn't mean they're the good guys." His hand tightened on hers. "This way."

The taillights of the SUV faded into the foggy darkness as they dashed across the asphalt toward the docks. There were four ships docked at the small port, including the *Xanadu Rose*. One was a barge, and one a tanker. The only remaining ship at the far end of the dock was a rusty behemoth stacked sky-high with containers.

"What are we looking for?" she asked.

"We know the *Xanadu* isn't where the women are being held hostage." Madrid's eyes scanned the ships as they walked the dock. "Another container ship would be my best bet."

The first ship they came to, the barge, was in the process of being unloaded. Huge cranes worked beneath massive spotlights.

They skirted the loading zone, sticking to the shadows on the opposite side of the low building. The next vessel was the tanker, with a foreign flag. Avoiding a street lamp, they passed the *Xanadu* and approached the final vessel. The massive ship was in poor condition, but even in the semidarkness Jess could make out the name emblazoned on the hull.

"The *Dorian Rae*," she whispered.

"Looks deserted."

"The perfect place to run an illegal smuggling operation."

"One way to find out."

Taking her hand, Madrid looked both ways, then sprinted toward the *Dorian Rae*. Jess found herself dragged into a dead run. The ship loomed as large as a mountain as they drew closer. Ropes as thick as a man's arm were secured to giant cleats set into concrete. She could hear waves slapping against the concrete piers. The massive vessel groaned like a ghost ship trying to free itself from its moorings.

They crossed to a primitive elevator used by shipping and U.S. Customs personnel, but the steel grid door was secured with a chain and padlock.

"What now?" Jess said.

"Piece of cake." Madrid dropped to his knees and dug into the duffel for the bolt cutters.

The chain snapped and clattered to the concrete. Giving her a look over his shoulder, Madrid slid open the door and stepped onto the platform. Fabricated with plywood and steel grid, the elevator had the appearance of being thrown together by less than talented construction workers. The only thing even remotely modern about it was the glowing Up button next to the door.

"Going up," Madrid muttered, and hit the button.

The car jolted and began its upward ascent. The wind whistled through the steel grid as the car climbed.

"What if someone sees us going up?" she asked.

"Let's hope that doesn't happen."

She was about to respond when a bell chimed and the elevator car jerked to a stop. When the door slid open, Jess started to move out of the car, but Madrid stopped her and went first. The elevator had opened onto a wide deck. Dead ahead, a dozen massive containers were stacked like giant toys. To Jess's left stood a building of sorts that soared another thirty feet into the night sky.

"Where are we?" she asked.

He looked around, then up. "I'd say we're standing just in front of the aft deckhouse."

A shudder moved through her as she looked around. Rusty and dilapidated, the ship looked as though it hadn't been used in a very long time. "This place gives me the creeps."

"Especially if you think about what might be happening onboard."

"What do we look for?"

"Anything suspicious. A locked door or padlock. Signs of recent use. It would be helpful if we could find where the women are being held captive."

"Or the women themselves."

He nodded.

"Do you think they're here?"

"If they're lucky," he said darkly. "Come on."

Drizzle floated down from a black sky as they made their way toward the front of the ship. Fog hovered at the deck level. Ahead, more decrepit containers were stacked like old cars awaiting the crusher.

They entered a walkway. Containers rose from the deck on either side, conveying the impression of a narrow canyon. Madrid climbed a scaffold that took him to one of the lower containers. He tried the door.

"Locked." He rapped his fist against steel. "Damn it."

There was no way they could reach the upper containers. But, honestly, Jess didn't think the containers looked like the kind of place where smugglers would stow human cargo. They were too out in the open.

"What about below deck?" she asked.

"Things could get dicey if we get caught below deck."

Jess knew he was having second thoughts about including her in this mission. While the realization that he was concerned for her safety warmed her, she couldn't let it keep them from doing what they'd come here to do.

"Madrid, we can't pass up this opportunity. We've gotten this far. Let's look around and see what we find."

When he looked at her, his expression was so torn that for a moment she wanted to reach out, touch him, tell him everything was going to be all right. But Jess knew better than to give in to that kind of temptation at a moment like this. Another kiss like the one he'd given her earlier and she might just lose her head.

"There's no one on this ship, Madrid."

"You don't know that."

"We can't leave empty-handed."

"Damn it, Jess, I don't want you to end up like Angela."

The words rendered her speechless. Up until

this moment he'd been operating on logic. Was it possible coolheaded Mike Madrid was experiencing some of the same emotions as she?

"Too many people I've cared about have ended up dead." He ground out the words as if to justify his earlier statement.

She did reach out then, a soft brush of her fingertips against his cheek. He winced as if her fingertips burned him. "Nothing is going to happen." She forced a smile she didn't feel. "We're the good guys, remember?"

"Sometimes that isn't enough."

"This time it has to be," she said.

He stared hard at her, nostrils flaring, his expression fraught with tension. "Fifteen minutes." His voice was so low she had to crane her neck forward to hear. "Then we're out of here even if I have to drag you. Believe me, I will."

Jess didn't doubt it, but there was no time to think of that now. "Let's go below deck."

Sighing as if in resignation, Madrid motioned toward the direction from which they'd come. "We passed a hatch a ways back. Follow me. Stay close."

The only sound came from the soft tap of their shoes against the steel deck. The hatch was set into the foremast platform. An oval steel door complete with a wheel lock and rubber seal. Jess kept watch while Madrid went to work on the lock. Two minutes and the hatch creaked open.

Madrid turned to her before entering. "If anything happens, I want you to get back up on deck. If you can't get off the ship, I want you to jump overboard and swim. Follow the lights."

For the first time, the reality of what they were doing hit home. A quiver of fear every bit as cold and deep as the water surrounding them ran the length of her. "We're not going to get caught."

"What we're doing is foolhardy, Jess." Giving her a final hard look, he slid the flashlight from the duffel and ducked through the hatch.

Descending into the bowels of the ship was like descending into hell. Only, this particular hell wasn't hot and fiery. It was cold and damp and dark. The odors of garbage and saltwater and diesel fuel filled the air as they reached the lower level.

The flashlight beam cut through the utter darkness to reveal a narrow horizontal corridor. Jess had never been claustrophobic, but she felt it pressing down on her now.

"This way."

Madrid's voice jerked her back from a place

she knew better than to go. He went left and she followed close behind him. Somewhere in the distance she heard water dripping. In her peripheral vision, when the beam hit just right, she could see droplets streaming down the rust-covered walls.

A distant scream shattered the silence. Jess froze, her heart leaping into a wild staccato. Vaguely she was aware of Madrid stopping, too, and the flashlight beam disappearing. The uneasiness she'd felt earlier grew into a slow and cold fear that wrapped around her like the fingers of death.

"What the hell was that?" she whispered into the darkness.

"Someone's on board. A female," came Madrid's voice. "And she's in trouble."

Judging from the terror resonating in the scream, the woman was more than in trouble.

She feared for her very life.

Chapter Eleven

"Where did it come from?"

Madrid flicked the flashlight back on. "Hard to tell. A lot of echo in here. Probably this level."

He shone the light between them, and Jess crossed to him on shaking legs. For the first time she questioned the wisdom of coming here. Maybe he was right. This was a suicide mission. No way were they going to pull this off without getting caught.

She thought of the scream and shuddered. "They're hurting someone," she said.

Grimacing, Madrid shook his head. "Sounded that way."

The thought made her sick. "We can't let this continue."

"I know. Damn it." He glanced at his watch. "We'll give ourselves ten minutes. After that, we turn around. No matter what. You got that?"

"I got it."

Keeping the beam low, Madrid took her down the cavelike corridor. Behind him, Jess noticed his free hand resting on the pistol tucked into his waistband, as if he were expecting someone to accost them at any moment.

Midway down the corridor, they came to another hatch. The wheel lock was affixed with a shiny new padlock and chain.

"Lock looks new," Jess said.

"Let's see what they have to hide." Madrid slid the bolt cutters out of the duffel. The steel snapped and the lock hit the floor before he could catch it. Casting her a tense look, he turned the wheel lock. Two turns. Three. He nearly had the hatch open when the thud of approaching footsteps sounded.

He doused the flashlight, plunging them into darkness. "Where are they coming from?"

Jess's heart revved like a race-car engine. She looked around wildly, but saw only the endless black void. "I don't know." Within the steel belly of the ship it was difficult to tell where sounds were coming from.

Around them, the ancient ship groaned like the walking dead. Water dripped incessantly. Seconds ticked into minutes, but they didn't move.

"They're gone," Madrid whispered.

She touched his shoulder. "Open the hatch."

Steel ground against steel as he turned the wheel lock. An instant later the airtight hatch hissed open. "We're in."

She jolted when his hand closed around her arm and guided her through the hatch. The darkness inside was so complete she couldn't see her hand even if she held it an inch in front of her face.

Jess nearly sighed in relief when the yellow beam of the flashlight flooded the room. Her relief was short-lived. The room wasn't a room at all, but more like a dungeon right out of some medieval castle, with shackles and chains welded to the steel walls. The flashlight beam didn't reveal much, but from where Jess stood she counted ten sets of shackles for wrists and ankles spaced about a foot apart. A drain was set into the floor. The stench of old urine hung heavy in the dank air.

"What the hell have we walked into?" Madrid muttered.

"A nightmare," Jess whispered.

He swept the beam around the large cell. A dozen bunk beds with paper-thin mattresses lined the far wall, four high and three across. A rusty sink and commode stood in the corner. Against the opposite wall a dozen more shackles and chains hung like macabre decorations.

"This is where the photo was taken," he said.

Jess jerked her attention to Madrid. "How do you know?"

"The sink is the same. See the rust stain?"

Jess had thought there was something familiar about the room. She hadn't been able to pinpoint what it was until he mentioned the sink. "You're right. But if this is the same place, where are the women?"

"This might explain some of it."

She looked over to see Madrid kneel. Her stomach heaved when the flashlight beam illuminated a shiny black stain on the floor, the size of a dinner plate. Even though the lighting was bad, Jess knew immediately it was blood.

"My God." She pressed a shaking hand to her stomach. "What is happening here?"

"Whatever it is, it's barbaric." Fury shone in his eyes when he rose. "And illegal as hell. I want photos of everything, including the stain on the floor. Hurry. We've only got a few minutes."

"Okay." She pulled the disposable camera from the duffel and snapped photos while he held the beam steady.

"The wall. Quickly," he said. "We don't have much time."

She jerked the camera to the wall, snapped half a dozen shots. She took a few more of the sink and commode. The bunks. The chains...

"These photos aren't definitive proof, but it will be enough to get an official investigation started."

"I thought Angela was already investigating."

"She was." He took the camera and dropped it back into the bag. "A lot of the stuff the MIDNIGHT Agency does is unofficial."

"What's the point?"

"The point is that sometimes things aren't as blac and white as they seem."

Jess wasn't exactly sure what he meant by that. The blood on the floor seemed about as black and white as anything she'd ever seen in her life. "What are you saying?"

"I'm saying there's probably more going on here than you or I know about."

"Like what?"

"Hard to say. Something international. Corruption on some level." He motioned toward the stain on the floor without looking at it. "One thing I can say for sure is that Angela would never let something so barbaric continue."

"Maybe that's why someone saw fit to stop her."

He scrubbed a hand over his face. "Yeah."

"Like who?"

"Someone with a lot at stake."

"Well, that certainly narrows it down." She spread her arms to encompass the terrible room. "Madrid, where does that leave us?"

His eyes drilled into hers. Within the depth of his gaze, she saw determination and tenacity and the strength of character to do the right thing no matter how difficult.

Or dangerous.

"Since I'm no longer with the agency, that leaves us with the freedom to do the right thing." He paused. "Even if it means crossing lines."

Jess wanted to ask him which lines he was talking about, but they were interrupted by the slam of a steel door. Madrid quickly clicked off the flashlight, total darkness crashing over them. Even with her heart hammering hard against her breast, Jess heard the pound of boots.

"Someone's coming this way," she whispered.

"More than one person." Taking her by the shoulders, he shoved her into the corridor. "Time to move. Fast."

He didn't give her time to think about it. His hand latched on to hers with the force of a vise grip. The next thing she knew she was being pulled forcefully down the corridor. They were midway to the hatch when overhead lights flashed on.

Horror whipped through her. A terrible sense of being exposed. Of danger. Vaguely she was aware of Madrid cursing under his breath. Of male voices shouting behind her. Heavy footsteps pounding steel. The sound of bullets being chambered.

"You, there! Halt! Now, or I'll fire!"

"Run!" came Madrid's voice.

He hit the hatch with both hands, but the steel didn't budge. "Help me crank this," he hissed.

Jess grabbed the wheel and spun it as hard as she could. But their efforts were in vain. She looked past Madrid to see three men rushing toward them, rifles thrust forward.

"Get your hands up and turn around slowly!"

Her hands shot into the air. Beside her, Madrid sighed. For an instant she feared he was going to do something crazy. Instead, he raised his hands and slowly turned. "Where the hell have you been?" he snapped.

A tall man with long blond hair pulled into

a ponytail sneered. "Who the hell are you and what are you doing here?"

Madrid frowned at the man as if he were dense. "I'm here to pick up my shipment, and so far all I've done is waste my time. Where the hell are the women?"

The three men exchanged looks.

The blond man lowered his rifle and stepped closer. Jess cringed when his pale blue eyes swept down the front of her, then to Madrid. "I asked you your name."

"David Collins," Madrid lied smoothly. "We've been waiting for an hour. Someone was supposed to meet us on deck, but no one showed."

Pale blue eyes landed on Jess. "Your name."

"T-Trish C-Cooper." She hoped her neighbor back in Phoenix didn't mind her using her name.

"This is a secure area. Off-limits to you."

Madrid made a sound of frustration. "Look, all I want is what I paid—"

Too quick for the eye to follow, the blond man spun the rifle and rammed the butt into Madrid's solar plexus. Air whooshed from his lungs and his knees buckled, hitting the floor with a thud.

Jess screamed, but before she could move the rifle came down a second time on the back of Madrid's neck with bone-crushing force. He reeled forward, would have gone down completely, but he broke his fall with his hands.

Jess knelt at his side. "My God, are you all right?"

When Madrid managed only a croak, she glared at the blond man. "Why did you do that?"

"I have no tolerance for liars," said the man.

Taking her lead from Madrid's earlier statements, Jess elaborated. "We were asked to come here. Something about a shipment. I don't know what kind of shipment and I don't care." She motioned toward Madrid. "We do not deserve this kind of treatment."

The blonde's lip curled. "I don't believe them."

The other two men exchanged looks.

Madrid raised his head. "Maybe you ought to check with your boss, Einstein," he said between gritted teeth. "While you're at it, tell him you're beating the hell out of his best customer."

The men shuffled their feet. The rifles were lowered, but only marginally. "Maybe we ought to call this in," said a muscle-bound man in a cheap blue suit.

Never taking his eyes from Madrid and Jess, the blond man worked a cell phone from his jacket pocket and punched in numbers.

Jess couldn't believe this was happening. They'd been so close to getting out. Next to her, Madrid was still on his hands and knees trying to catch his breath. That was when she spotted the bulge of the pistol at the small of his back. Her heart banged like a jackhammer against her ribs. Even though they were out-numbered, she wondered if he had a plan. If he was buying time. If he was going to do some-thing nuts…

While the blonde spoke into the phone, the third man motioned toward Madrid with his rifle. "Search him."

The man in the blue suit stepped forward. Setting his boot against Madrid's back, he leaned forward and yanked the pistol from his waist-band. "My, my, my, what do we have here?"

"Protection against thugs like you," Jess said. But in the back of her mind she was wondering what was going to happen when they found the duffel with the camera and other incriminating items inside. Last time she'd seen it, the bag had been tied to Madrid's belt. A covert glance told her it was no longer there. Where was it? Had he ditched it when he realized they weren't going to get away?

"I'll cuff him," the third man said to the man

in the blue suit. Then he looked at Jess. "Search her."

Another wave of dread swamped her. Jess knew once Madrid was bound there would be no escaping whatever these monsters had planned.

The man in the blue suit leered at Jess, his grin revealing stained teeth. "That'll be my pleasure."

Jess gasped when he gripped her arm and yanked her to her feet. "Put your hands up and spread those pretty legs of yours," he said in a gruff voice.

Next to her, Madrid straightened just as the third man reached into his pocket. Jess spotted nylon restraints and her heart went wild in her chest.

"Cuff him." The man in the blue suit licked his lips, his eyes flicking to Jess. "Then we'll have us some fun."

His eyes were alight with some dark anticipation she did not want to think about. Dread rose in her chest when she realized both she and Madrid would soon be at their mercy.

"I said put your hands up," the man in the blue suit ordered. "*Now.*"

Feeling trapped and vulnerable, Jess looked around. But there was no one to come to their rescue. Even if Madrid managed to avoid the cuffs and get to his feet, they were outmanned and outgunned.

There was no escape.

Heart pounding, she raised her hands to shoulder height. "I'm unarmed. You don't need to search me." She tried to make her voice sound strong, but her throat was so tight she managed little more than a whisper.

The man in the blue suit put down Madrid's pistol and stepped toward her. "I think I'll just check for myself. You look like a woman who's got lots of hiding places."

Jess could tell by the glint in his eyes that once he put his hands on her he wasn't going to stop with a simple search.

In her peripheral vision she saw Madrid holding his stomach and struggling to his feet. The third man stood behind him, ready to snap the cuffs into place. But Jess could plainly see that both men's attention was on her. Running his tongue over his lips, he slowly patted her down. The outside of her thighs. Her calves. Then he began working his way back up.

The man's hands paused just below her breasts. Jess forced herself to make eye contact. "Don't," she said.

The man's eyes glinted like a rat's. "Who's going to stop me?"

Madrid moved so fast and unexpectedly that Jess didn't have time to get out of the way. The man in the blue suit brought up his rifle, but he wasn't fast enough. Madrid thrust his arm forward and she heard a loud crack. The other man went rigid and an instant later collapsed, his body convulsing.

Jess didn't know what was happening. The only information her brain processed was that Madrid had some kind of weapon that was quickly evening the odds. The blond man dropped the phone and grabbed for his rifle, but Madrid kicked the barrel. An errant gunshot exploded as Madrid tagged the blonde. Electric current snapped through the air hitting the blond man and knocking him to the floor.

Jess spun to the other man, but she wasn't fast enough. He dived at her and wrapped his left arm around her while going for the pistol with his right hand.

"Madrid!" she screamed. "Gun!"

The force of his body slamming into hers knocked her off her feet. As she fell, all Jess could think about was getting to the gun, keeping him from shooting Madrid. She twisted in midair. In her peripheral vision she spotted Madrid rushing toward them. She glimpsed his furious dark eyes, his lips pulled back into a snarl.

The gun came up, leveled on Madrid.

Oh, dear God, no!

Acting on impulse, she thrust the heel of her hand at the pistol. The barrel shifted and the gun exploded inches from her ear, deafening her. As if in slow motion Madrid aimed his palm-size weapon at the man. Another loud crack rent the air. The man's body went rigid, an animalistic sound tearing from his throat.

The next thing Jess knew she was lying on the floor, trying to catch her breath. Her ears were ringing, her body felt as if it had been run over by a tank and she couldn't stop shaking.

"Easy." Strong arms pulled her to her feet. "Didn't mean to hit you with that."

Madrid, she thought dazedly, and reached for him. "What happened?"

Setting his hand against her cheek, he ducked his head and met her gaze. "You got your feet under you?"

Jess hadn't quite decided, but she nodded. "What is that in your hand?"

He brandished the small object. "Mini stun gun."

The weapon was the size of a garage door opener. Judging from the three men laid out on the floor, it packed a hell of a lot more punch. "You hit me with it?"

"Current went through the goon and into you." He rubbed his thumb against her cheek. "I'm sorry about that."

If she hadn't been so shaken, so terrified, Jess might have been angry; she might even have laughed. At the moment all she wanted to do was get out of there.

"Where on earth did you get it?" she asked.

"It was in Angela's bag of tricks."

"Pretty high-tech."

"And then some."

The sound of footsteps punctuated the statement. Madrid looked over his shoulder, his expression turning grave. "We're going to have to split up."

"No."

Grasping her arms, he gave her a gentle shake, his gaze seeking hers. "Listen to me, Jess. Trust me. I know what I'm doing."

The last thing Jess wanted to do was split up, but her instincts told her to trust Madrid. Maybe because she knew he was the kind of man who would sacrifice himself to keep her safe. At the moment she didn't know if that was good or bad.

Grabbing his pistol from the floor, he chambered a bullet and handed it to her. "It's ready to go. Use it if you need to. Don't trust anyone but me."

Without giving her time to debate, he spun her around, shoved her in the direction from which they'd come. "Run. Get back on deck, then get off the ship any way you can."

Jess risked a look back at him. He'd started in the direction of the footsteps. "You can't walk right into the lion's den," she said.

He grinned. "The lion's den is my specialty," he replied, and disappeared down the darkened hall.

THE CORRIDORS CREAKED like the underbelly of some ancient, arthritic beast. Jess's sneakers pounded against the steel floor as she ran down the corridor. At some point flashing red lights had come on as if to signal some kind of emergency—or, in this case, a security breach.

She ran as she had never run before. Terror followed her every step of the way. She could hear her breaths echoing off the walls. She passed several hatches, but couldn't remember which one she and Madrid had entered. She was afraid to stop. Afraid the men with guns would find her and kill her...or worse.

Run. Get back on deck, then get off the ship any way you can.

Madrid's words reverberated inside her head. If only she could remember how to reach the deck.

Another corridor veered right. Jess stopped, vacillated. She tried hard to remember if they'd come that way, but couldn't. She wasn't familiar with the ship's layout. In the flashing lights, everything looked the same. In the back of her mind she wondered how Madrid was faring.

Behind her, the sound of leather soles against steel sent her heart into her throat. Down the hall. Too close for comfort. Jess took the corridor, threw herself into an all-out sprint. All the while she could hear the footsteps getting closer, the men gaining on her.

She passed another corridor, ducked into it without forethought and found herself in a stairwell landing. Steel grid steps led down and up. She went up, taking the steps two at a time. Somewhere behind her a hatch slammed and shouting echoed all around her.

She passed another landing, the door to which was marked Minus One. She used the steel rail to fling herself around the corner. Her legs burned as she took the next flight up, but she didn't stop. The next door was marked Zero. Jess attacked the wheel lock, spun it as fast as she could. Steel creaked when she shoved it open.

Relief poured through her when cold and rain met her face. All she could think was that she'd made it out of hell. Her relief was short-lived, though, as the beam of a spotlight flashed by. Thrusting herself through the door, Jess looked around and tried to get her bearings. Several spotlights had come on since she and Madrid had gone below deck. Silhouetted against the night sky, she saw the deckhouse and realized she'd somehow run the length of the ship. If she remembered correctly, they had entered near the deckhouse.

To her right, a cable rail denoted the edge of the ship. To her left was a small, lighted structure, one side of which was lined with fifty-gallon drums. Several wooden pallets were stacked neatly along the other side. Planning to use the drums and pallets as cover, Jess left the hatch. Her heart pounded as she crossed an open area.

If the spotlight landed on her here, she would be in plain sight.

She barely noticed the rain soaking her as she neared the pallets. She was a few feet away when sudden bright light blinded her. An authoritative male voice penetrated the fog of terror.

"Halt! Put your hands up! *Now!*"

Instinct kicked in. Jess spun and bolted. She didn't know where she was going. All she knew was if they caught her, they would kill her.

"Stop or I'll shoot!"

The words were punctuated by the *thunk, thunk, thunk* of gunfire. A pallet less than a foot away from her exploded. Disbelief and terror tore through her.

She crossed the deck at a reckless speed. Rain and wind blinded her, but she didn't slow down. She could hear the men behind her, their angry shouts rising above the din of rain.

She reached the rail. To her left she saw men racing toward her, flashlight beams bobbing. To her right was another small building, with a closed hatch. Was it locked?

"Put your hands up now!"

Get off the ship any way you can.

Madrid's words came to her like a beacon out of the darkness. Jess knew what she had to do.

Her legs shook violently as she hauled herself over the rail. More shouting sounded behind her, but she barely heard it over her wildly pounding heart.

She looked into the black abyss of the bay below. It was so dark she couldn't even tell how far the fall would be. All she could do now was pray it didn't kill her.

"Stop!"

Closing her eyes, Jess said a silent prayer and flung herself into the darkness.

Chapter Twelve

The water slapped her like a giant icy hand, then swallowed her whole. The impact knocked the breath from her lungs; the cold stole what little she had left.

It was like being sucked into a bottomless, icy abyss. Every sense in her body screamed with shock. She didn't know how deep she'd gone. Didn't know what horrors lay above—or below. The only thing she knew for certain at the moment was that she wanted to live.

Jess kicked with all her might, but her clothes and shoes felt like lead weights. She didn't know if she was making any progress, but the alternative to drowning was too horrendous to contemplate.

She broke the surface a moment later, choking and coughing. Rain and wind buffeted her. A wave swamped her and she swallowed a mouthful of the sea. She tasted saltwater and panic and the hard edge of her own fear. In the back of her mind she wondered if Madrid had gotten off the ship. If he had survived. If she would ever see him again. The thought of him gave her the strength she needed.

Treading water, she looked around and tried to get her bearings. Above her the ship rose out of the water like a steel iceberg. A single spotlight shone down, but it was a good fifty feet away from where she'd fallen. They were looking for her. That meant she didn't have much time.

Turning, she spotted the concrete pier twenty yards away. Jutting ten feet out of the water, it would be a tough climb. But Jess thought there would probably be places she could get a grip or maybe a dangling rope she could grab.

The swim to the pier seemed to take forever. The cold was quickly zapping her strength. Once the searchlight from the ship came within ten feet of her and she had to duck beneath the surface. She knew sharks were the least of her worries, taking into consideration the men with semiautomatic weapons, but the entire time she couldn't stop thinking about all the unsavory creatures lurking in the deep.

By the time her hands made contact with the

concrete, she wasn't sure she had the strength to pull herself out of the water. For several seconds she clung to the pier, shaking with cold and exhaustion, gasping for breath. Her teeth chattered as she looked around.

There were still lights visible aboard the *Dorian Rae,* but the spotlights had been doused. Did that mean they'd stopped looking for her? Where was Madrid?

Knowing the water was stealing her body heat and strength at an alarming rate, Jess maneuvered along the barnacle-covered pier until she came to a rope hanging down from an old bumper float. Now, if she could find the strength to pull herself up and out of the water.

A scream tore from her throat when something large brushed against her. *Shark* was the only thought her mind processed. She lunged at the rope, but before she could reach it a hand slapped over her mouth.

"Easy, Jess, it's me."

Several terror-filled seconds passed before the words registered. Before the familiar voice soothed the jagged ends of her nerves. When he removed his hand from her mouth, Jess choked out a sound of pure relief. "Madrid…"

"Are you hurt?"

"N-no. J-just c-cold."

He looked around. "I'm going to get you out of here."

She reached for the rope. "We can climb out."

He eased her back into the icy water. The urge to fight him was strong; more than anything, she wanted out of the water. But his words stopped her. "We're less than ten yards from the port police. You climb out here and you'll get a bullet for your trouble."

That convinced her.

"Hold on to me," he said quietly.

She glanced over at him to find his eyes already on hers. Without hesitating, she hooked a finger around his belt loop.

"Like this," he said, taking both her hands in his and wrapping them around his waist. He motioned to his right. "I'm taking you over to that old boat ramp."

She hadn't noticed the ramp until she followed his gesture. The concrete was crumbling and fraught with weeds as high as a man's waist. But it was the easiest way out of the water. The weeds would provide some cover.

He shoved away from the pier, and she felt the muscles beneath her palms tighten as he began to swim. Jess kicked her feet in an effort to help, but her legs felt as if they were weighted down. Her feet were numb. The icy water felt like razors against her skin. At some point she had stopped shaking. It was as if she had floated out of her body and was looking down, watching two strangers struggle through the cold, black water.

It took only a few minutes for him to reach the boat ramp, but it felt like hours. He stepped onto the concrete. "Easy."

Jess hadn't realized she was still clinging to him. But when she let go, she sank back into the water. Exhaustion tugged at her and the darkness beckoned, offered a place that was warm and safe.

"Bloody hell."

Madrid's voice reached her as if from a great distance. "Whas wrong?" Surprise rippled through her when her words slurred.

"Cold got you. You're hypothermic."

"I'm 'kay." But no matter how hard she tried, she couldn't get her legs under her.

Strong arms wrapped around her. The next thing she knew she was being swept into his arms. She wanted to ask him what he was doing and where he was taking her, but her mouth had suddenly forgotten how to speak. Her mind felt fuzzy and confused; she couldn't seem to pull her thoughts together.

Vaguely she was aware of him carrying her across the weed-riddled asphalt. She worried about the men from the ship spotting them as he shoved her into the car. But she figured neither of them was in any shape to do anything about it. She heard the engine start and saw Madrid looking into the rearview mirror.

And then like the water that had nearly stolen her life, she slipped into the darkness and floated away.

MADRID TOOK HER to the only place he could think of. As an agent, he had several refuges. Secret places nobody knew about except him. The RV wasn't his favorite, but it was secluded, mobile and safe. For now it would have to do.

He was all too aware how dangerous hypothermia was. He'd lost a fellow agent to it while on assignment some five years ago. Cold and water were silent killers that could steal a life like thieves in the night. There was no way he was going to let it take Jess.

She seemed weightless as he carried her to the RV and took her up the steps. Unlocking the door, he shoved it open. The place smelled stale, but it was dry and warm. For now that would have to be enough.

He set her on the small settee. She spilled from his arms in a wet heap. "Hang on, babe," he whispered. "I'll be right back."

Quickly he went outside to the generator at the rear of the RV. It started on the first try. Madrid kept all his equipment in working order. In his line of business, he never knew when he would need it, and he was intimately acquainted with Murphy's Law.

Back inside the RV, he switched on the lights and felt alarm shoot through him when he saw the pale cast to Jess's complexion. She had no color whatsoever, except for her lips, which were tinged blue. "Damn."

Not giving himself time to debate, he began to work the wet clothing from her body. His hands shook as he tugged the soggy sweatshirt over her head. She thrashed and tried to push him away, but Madrid gently set her back down. "Easy," he said. "I need to get you dry and warm."

"G'way."

"Not a chance."

But his hands hesitated. Jess was stripped down to her jeans and bra. As vulnerable as a woman could be. This was no time for him to notice the silky white flesh of her abdomen or that her limbs were long and lean, just the way he liked. They were in the midst of a life-threatening emergency. But as he reached for the snap of her jeans, he noticed all of those things and more.

She shoved at him as he worked her zipper down. "Don't."

"I've got to get you warm," he said, brushing her hands away.

Wide hips and a flat belly came into view. He gritted his teeth against the hard tug of attraction that coiled low in his gut. The hot rise of lust made him feel like a lecher. But while Madrid had always considered himself a professional, he'd never denied he was a man with weaknesses.

"Don't go there, partner," he muttered.

But he already had. He'd stripped her down to her bra and panties and for the span of a full minute he could do nothing but stand there and drink in her beauty.

Shaken by his reaction to her, he gave himself a hard mental shake. She needed warmth and rest, not some burned-out federal agent ogling her while she was only semiconscious.

"That's bottom-of-the-barrel low, Madrid," he growled, and started for the overhead locker off the tiny head. He pulled two blankets and a pillow from the shelf and went back to the settee. She stirred when he slid the pillow beneath her cheek, but she didn't open her eyes. Probably a good thing, since he'd end up getting lost in them.

Only when he'd finished covering her with both blankets did he realize his own condition wasn't much better. He'd been running on autopilot since leaving the shipyard, but the cold had sapped his strength. He felt as if he were moving through a fog. If some goon with a gun came calling, he wasn't in any shape to do much about it.

Leaving Jess on the settee, Madrid stripped, let his clothes drop to the floor and stepped into the shower. The water wasn't yet hot, but it was warm enough to get his body temperature back to normal. For now that was the best he could hope for.

He raised his face to the spray and felt his muscles begin to melt. He knew he should be thinking about solving the mystery surrounding Angela's death. About how he was going to handle the end of his career.

But he couldn't get Jess out of his mind. He couldn't get the picture of her out of his head.

The image of his hands roaming milky flesh. The sounds of her sighs when he touched her. The way it might feel running his fingers through her silky hair...

He had it bad for her. As far as the MIDNIGHT Agency was concerned, she was a fugitive from justice. He wondered if Sean Cutter had figured it out yet. If his relationship with Jess would expedite his fall from grace.

"First you gotta make it through the night," he muttered, and turned his face toward the spray.

EVERYTHING HE'D EVER WORKED for was falling apart. A business endeavor he'd been working on for nearly a decade. A business that had afforded him a lifestyle he otherwise would never even have dreamed of.

All because of some two-bit federal agent and Jess Atwood. A freaking waitress, of all things.

They had been on board the *Dorian Rae*. In custody, in fact. But his men had screwed up, and now they were free. He could only assume they knew everything. That they were dangerously close to blowing sky-high everything he'd worked for.

A knock at the door drew his attention. "It's open," he snapped.

The man in the uniform entered the elegantly appointed office overlooking San Francisco Bay. "We've got problems."

"Judging from the way things went down last night, we've got a damn train wreck on our hands." Leaning back in his high-back leather chair, he glared at the cop. "How in the name of God could you let things get this far?"

"I've got my best men on it."

"Some of my clientele are getting impatient. They're getting nervous. Nervous customers don't pay."

"I just need some time—"

"We don't have any more time!" Pulling himself back, he set his hands on the desk and laced his fingers. "She's a waitress, for God's sake."

The other man flushed. "It's the agent who's causing the problems."

"I don't need to have problems pointed out to me. I need them solved, and I need them solved yesterday. Do you understand?"

"We're doing everything we can."

"And once again you've proven yourself incompetent."

When he saw the other man's eyes go hard, he reminded himself that this man could be dangerous if pushed too hard, so he decided to ease up. Once the crisis was over, he'd deal with him. For now, all he cared about was salvaging the project and his reputation.

"Let me make some calls," he said. "Call in some markers."

The cop shot him a questioning look. "What kind of markers?"

"A marker that might help me get Madrid out of the picture once and for all."

The uniformed man nodded. "In the interim, what do you want me to do?"

"I want you to find them." He picked up the phone. "When you do, I want you to kill them both."

Chapter Thirteen

Jess woke with a start. For an instant she lay nestled in the warmth of the blankets. But while her body cried out for more sleep, her mind began to churn. The memory of everything that had happened the night before rushed back. Entering the *Dorian Rae*. Finding the prisonlike cells. Hearing the scream echo through the corridors. Running through dark and narrow passageways. The icy slap of the water when she'd jumped overboard to avoid capture.

Everything else was a blur. She didn't remember taking a bump on the head, but her memory was foggy. She had a vague recollection of Madrid speaking to her, gazing at her with concern in his eyes. Then nothing...

She looked around. Her surroundings were not familiar, but she was pretty sure she was in some kind of RV. There was a small galley.

A bench seat and fold-down tabletop. Faux paneling. A narrow door she assumed led outside. Someone had covered her with blankets.... Then she remembered. But Madrid was nowhere in sight.

A quick physical inventory told her she was unhurt, except for some sore muscles and a lingering fatigue. She snuggled more deeply into the blankets, comfort turning to shock when she realized she was wearing only her panties and bra.

But she knew. Madrid had undressed her. Again. Her clothes had been wet, after all. It wasn't as if he could leave her in them all night. Still, the thought of him seeing her without her clothes made her cheeks heat.

"Morning."

She sat up abruptly at the sound of his voice. He was standing in the doorway, a grocery bag in his arm. "I didn't hear you come in," she said.

"I thought you might like some lunch," he said. "It's been a while since we ate."

"Where are we?"

"In a safe place." His gaze flicked over her, then he met her eyes. "How are you feeling?"

"Okay." The image of him undressing her came to her unbidden. Jess tightened her hand on the blanket she clutched to her chest and hoped he didn't notice the blush. "I remember going into the water. I don't remember much afterward."

"By the time I pulled you out, you were hypothermic. Semiconscious. I got you to the car and brought you here."

"Thank you." She looked around. "Where is here?"

"An RV park and campground a few miles from the coast."

She nodded, pursed her lips. "And my clothes?"

"In the dryer." He set the bag on the counter in the galley. "I'll get them for you and then fix us something to eat. Then we need to talk."

"I want to take a shower."

"In that case, let me run the engine for a few minutes. It's faster than the generator." Turning from her, he opened a small cabinet above the dining table and pulled a set of keys from a hook inside. "Water will be hot in ten minutes."

When Jess finally got in the shower, the hot water felt delicious cascading over her sore muscles, and she couldn't get enough of it. By the time she turned off the faucets, the water was beginning to run cold.

She found Madrid in the galley. He'd pulled

down a fold-out table and set out paper plates. "I made omelets. I hope that's okay."

Jess's stomach grumbled at the sight of the omelet neatly folded on her plate. Next to it was a large glass of orange juice and two slices of toast. "Nice."

He poured coffee into a plastic cup and handed it to her, his dark eyes meeting hers. "I wouldn't go that far."

Jess took the cup, but she didn't take her eyes from his. He had the longest lashes of any male she'd ever met. "You didn't tell me you cooked."

"I haven't told you a lot of things."

"I bet."

He grinned at her over his cup.

She smiled back. "You must have a lot of hidden talents."

"You have no idea."

She wasn't sure where the banter was coming from. Something to break the tension and stress of the past few days. After all, it wasn't as if they didn't have more important things to discuss. Like what they were going to do about the horrors they'd discovered on board the *Dorian Rae*.

Gathering her thoughts, she took the bench

seat at the settee. He sat across from her and they delved into their food.

It was strange sitting down for something as mundane as a quiet meal. Jess couldn't remember the last time she'd eaten; in the past few days she'd been too scared to even think of it. But looking at the omelet, she was suddenly famished.

Midway through the meal, however, the questions buzzing around in her head would wait no longer. "What are we going to do about what we found last night?"

Madrid forked some of the egg. "Well, we know the Lighthouse Point PD is involved in human smuggling."

"Not to mention murder."

"Goes hand in hand."

Thinking of Angela, Jess shook her head. "How do we stop them?"

"We find the head of the operation and cut it off."

"Someone with the Lighthouse Point PD?"

"Could be, but I doubt it. This is a big operation, Jess. Far-reaching. International. A lot of people are involved. The Lighthouse Point PD simply allows them to operate in the bay."

"They get paid to look the other way."

"Those photos we took last night would

have helped." He grimaced. "The camera was in the duffel, though, and I lost the duffel when we got ambushed."

"If they find it, can they ID you?"

He gave her a wry smile. "I'm too careful for that, but we could have used the tools outside." A sigh hissed between his lips. "The *Dorian Rae* is key. I need to find out who owns and operated the ship."

"How do we do that?"

"I put in a call earlier this morning." He set his hand against the cell phone clipped to his belt.

"The MIDNIGHT Agency."

"Yeah."

She thought about that a moment. "Are the police still looking for me?"

"You're a person of interest."

"In other words, I'm still a suspect."

His gaze met hers. "You'd be a hell of a lot safer if I turned you over to the feds."

Surprise rippled through her that he would even think of it. "We've been over that, Madrid."

"And my stance on it hasn't changed."

"If I let myself be taken in, you'll lose your ace in the hole."

A hard glint entered his eyes. "You turn yourself in and I won't have to worry about some goon sneaking in here in the middle of the night and cutting your throat."

She hoped he didn't see the shudder that ran through her. "Or I can spend the next week sitting in a jail cell while Angela's real killer is covering his tracks and working to frame me."

"You know I won't let that happen."

A rise of anger shot through her. "I have no intention—"

A knock at the door made them both jump up. Drawing his pistol, Madrid crossed to the door. "Yeah?"

"It's Vanderpol. Open up."

Madrid's hand slid away from the gun. He opened the door, leaned against the jamb. "About time."

A tall man with military-short hair shook the rain from his trench and stepped inside. Dark, intelligent eyes swept from Madrid to her, then back to Madrid. "Cutter will send me to Siberia if he finds out I met with you."

"I'll be lucky to wind up in Antarctica."

"Can't argue with that." His eyes sliding back to Jess, he extended his hand. "Jake Vanderpol."

His hand was large and rough as it encompassed hers. "Jessica Atwood."

He grasped her hand for an instant too long,

then released it and turned to Madrid. "I got the information you needed."

A silent communication passed between the two men. Jess suddenly felt like an outsider.

"She knows." Madrid motioned to the table and settee.

Jess sat. Madrid slid in beside her.

"Okay." Vanderpol took the bench opposite them and tugged a small notebook from the pocket of his trench. "The *Dorian Rae* is owned by a shipping conglomerate based in San Francisco called Capricorn Intercontinental Shipping."

"Owner?"

"High roller by the name of Gabriel Capricorn."

"Clean?"

"Not squeaky, but not quite dirty enough to head up a human smuggling ring."

"If not Capricorn, then who?"

"I got a hit on his VP. Slick guy by the name of Randall Yates."

"What kind of hit?"

"Got busted in 1997 for smuggling in ten illegals from China."

"Female?"

"Yup."

"Conviction?"

"During trial, eight of the women testified that they were stowaways."

"And the other two?"

"Disappeared off the face of the earth."

Madrid seemed to digest the words, his expression dark and thoughtful. "He was acquitted?"

"Yup. And get this. He used to run a shipping corporation out of Seattle. Owned a couple of massage parlors."

"Interesting combination."

"It is if you consider who worked the booths."

"Don't tell me. Illegal immigrants."

"Mostly from China. Immigration busted him a dozen times but he always beat the rap. Cost of doing business, I guess."

"Prostitution?"

"He was never charged, but if the shoe fits..." Jake lifted his shoulder, let it fall.

"When did he hook up with Capricorn?"

"Two years ago."

"Sounds like a match made in heaven."

"Or hell, depending on your perspective."

The two men fell silent. Jess's mind spun with everything she'd heard. It was as if the pieces of the puzzle were finally coming together. "So how do we stop them?" she asked.

Both heads turned to her simultaneously. Looking into their eyes, Jess knew they were going to try to shut her out. Because she was a woman. Because they were professionals and she wasn't. The reasons didn't matter. She wasn't going to let them do it.

"Angela was my friend," she said. "These people tried to frame me. They tried to kill me. They tried to kill Nicolas. I need to do this."

The two men exchanged looks, and Jess got a bad feeling in the pit of her stomach. Her worst fears were solidified when Madrid addressed her. "I want you to go back with Jake. Ride this out from a safe place."

"No." Anger surged. Jess rose abruptly. "Don't try to shut me out of this."

"You can help from MIDNIGHT headquarters."

She shot Madrid a furious stare. "Don't patronize me."

He rose. "Jess, you're going to have to trust me. Please. You're more of a hindrance than a help here."

"I'm a hindrance because you're so obsessed with locking me out that you haven't even considered using me as bait."

The RV went silent. In her peripheral vision

Jess saw Vanderpol's gaze flick from her to Madrid. But Madrid never took his eyes off her. His laugh was fraught with annoyance and incredulity. "No dice."

"They think I can ID Angela's killer. They think Nicolas saw it. Or maybe they think he told me who it was. Whatever the case, they want me dead."

"No."

"You know it's the best way to smoke out these bastards. Maybe the only way."

"I know it's the best way to get you dead!" he shouted.

She blinked, surprised by the vehemence behind the words. Knowing that for whatever reason she wasn't going to get through to him, she turned her attention to Vanderpol. "Dangle me in front of them and they'll bite."

Vanderpol's expression revealed nothing of what he was thinking or feeling. But he didn't say no.

Madrid, on the other hand, wasted no time with his refusal. He crossed to her, wrapped his fingers around her arms. "I know what these people are capable of, Jess. I've seen their handiwork. They're brutal and savage and I won't let you end up like Angela."

"Then let me do this." When he only stared at her, she lifted her hand. "Let me help, damn it."

He winced when her palm brushed his cheek. Grasping her wrist, he lowered it to her side. "I won't be the one to sign your death warrant," he said, and walked away.

JAKE VANDERPOL and Mike Madrid stood outside the RV in the lightly falling rain. "You sure she's not involved?" Jake asked.

"She didn't kill Angela, if that's what you're asking." Madrid shot him a hard look. "I'll bet my life on it."

"You might just be doing that, partner."

Madrid was getting wet, but he didn't care. He was too annoyed. Too damned worried about Jess. He felt as if he were losing control of the situation. He knew firsthand there was no better way to get someone hurt. Why the hell couldn't she just cooperate?

"You might consider taking her up on her offer."

Madrid's gaze jerked to Jake's. Anger swept through him that the other man would even suggest it. "I don't want those bastards any-where near her."

Jake frowned. "Look, Madrid, it's none of

my business, but it seems to me you're not thinking clearly about any of this."

"I'm thinking clearly enough to know if I dangle Jess or the boy in front of these bastards there's a damn good chance I won't get them back."

"Cutter thought it was a good idea."

Realization reared up inside Jake, followed by another quick punch of anger. "Cutter knew you were coming here."

"He knows a lot of things."

"Did he ask you to try to talk me into using them, Jake?"

That the other man couldn't meet his gaze was all the answer Madrid needed. "Cutter can go straight to hell."

Jake did meet his gaze then. "This is about keeping things in perspective, Madrid. Think about it. You have a key that could stop untold misery. Yet you're unwilling to use it because of something that happened a long time ago."

"Shut up about that."

"These bastards could be bringing in hundreds of women a year. God only knows how many of them don't make the journey. You have the power to stop it, but you won't."

"I won't risk an innocent woman's life to do

it. If that's what you want, then you can go to hell, too."

Unfazed by the remark, Jake shook his head. "You're screwing up, my man."

"These bastards murder indiscriminately. What the hell do you expect me to do?"

"I expect you to be a professional." Jake closed the distance between them and jabbed a finger into Madrid's chest. "Evidently you're too wrapped up in having sex to manage."

"This isn't about sex, damn it."

"Yeah, well, I hope she's worth it, because you're an inch away from kissing your career goodbye."

For several tense minutes the only sound came from the tinkle of rain against dry leaves and the rustle of wind through the trees. "You know as well as I do the woman and that kid are your best bet for smoking these bastards out of their holes," Jake said finally.

Madrid shook his head. "I'll find another way."

"For your sake, I hope you can."

At that, Jake Vanderpol turned and walked away.

Chapter Fourteen

The RV smelled of her when he walked inside. A light, airy scent that reminded him of summer meadows and wildflowers. A scent that made him long for something elusive and put a knot in his gut because he knew it was the one thing he could never have.

Hanging his jacket in the cubbyhole beside the door, he headed to the stove to make coffee.

"What were you two talking about?"

Madrid turned to see her standing in the hall just outside the lavatory. She'd pulled her hair into a ponytail, revealing a long and slender throat. Staring at her, all he could think was that he wanted to put his mouth on her.

"Agency stuff." His voice came out as a growl as he turned back to the stove. He didn't want to face her feeling like this. He knew one touch from her and he would do something he'd regret for the rest of his life.

"You know he's right."

He stiffened. "I know using you or Nicolas as bait would be the fastest way to get you both killed." Coffee forgotten, he turned to face her. "Are you willing to risk his life?"

"Not his." She stared at him, her gaze unflinching. "Mine."

"No way."

"You'd rather have countless young women dying?"

"I'd rather find a better way."

"There is no better way!" she shouted abruptly. "Damn it, I want my life back. I want to feel safe. I want Nicolas to be safe. I want the bastards responsible for Angela's death to pay for what they did."

Suddenly furious, Madrid crossed the space between them. Grasping her upper arms, he shook her. "I will not have another death on my conscience!" he roared.

Jess blinked, opened her mouth to speak, but said nothing. Seconds later she managed, "What?"

He hadn't meant to say it. Dredging up the past was the last thing he needed, especially with a woman who was all too willing to lay it on the line. For the span of several heartbeats he stood there, holding her arms, his heart pounding.

She stared back at him, her eyes wide and startled. "What are you talking about?"

Until this moment he hadn't realized the root of his resistance to using her as bait. The source of the knot in his gut. Over the past five years he'd learned to live with it. He'd learned to use it as part of what drove him to do his job and do it well.

"Madrid, talk to me."

He didn't want to discuss it. He didn't want to reveal his greatest fear. His deepest agony. Or the deep, dark pit that was his past. But looking into her eyes, he knew she wasn't going to let it go.

Releasing her, he let his hands slide down her arms. "Let it go, Jess."

He started to turn away, but she stopped him. "Whose death are you talking about?"

"Not just one life." Slowly he turned to face her. "Two lives. Two innocent people gone forever. Both deaths were my fault."

Outside, the rain had begun to drum, now pounding hard against the sheet-metal roof. Inside, his heart kept perfect time, increasing with the torrent.

"Who?" she asked.

"It doesn't matter."

"It matters to me."

He didn't want to say the words. Even though five years had passed, they still ripped open something inside him. "My wife and child."

For a moment she just stood there, staring at him, her eyes wide and filled with pain. Not for herself. For him. He didn't want her sympathy. He sure as hell didn't want her pity. All he wanted was to keep her safe, because he couldn't bear the thought of her being hurt because of him.

"I'm sorry," she said.

"It's done. In the past." He grimaced. "I'm a wiser man for it."

She seemed to consider that for a moment. "I can't see you being at fault for something like that. You're too careful. Too good at what you do."

"I wasn't five years ago." The smile that curved his mouth was sharp. "One day all that recklessness caught up with me."

In the worst possible way, a little voice reminded him.

"Tell me," she whispered.

Madrid could feel himself shutting down, withdrawing, his emotions closing up like a box.

It was what he did, and he did it well. He insulated himself against hurt, erected a wall to protect his heart. The protective mechanisms had kept him sane for five years. "Some other time."

He knew she was going to come to him. He saw intent in her eyes. And knew what would happen if she touched him. He could feel the need churning inside him, the ever-present knot in his gut tightening, the old recklessness roiling like a wild sea.

When she set her palm against his cheek he jolted, besieged by the urge to pull back to a safe distance. But the part of him that was a man—the part that had been alone for five long years—was stronger than the need to protect himself.

"Don't." He ground out the words.

But Jess didn't stop. Rising on her tiptoes, she pressed her mouth first to his cheek, then to his mouth. It was only a light, comforting peck, but Madrid's heart began to pound. He stood stone still and endured the intimate contact. But his resistance wouldn't last. And when his control broke, it would be violent and powerful enough to sweep both of them away.

God help them both when that happened, because if Madrid was certain of one thing in this world, it was that everything he touched—everything he loved—died.

As the pleasure of her kiss melted the steel surrounding his heart, he vowed he would never love Jessica Atwood.

JESS KNEW BETTER than to let the moment get physical. Neither of them was in any frame of mind to be considering any kind of relationship, physical or otherwise.

But the womanly part of her scoffed at the idea of turning the other cheek. Somehow she had to get through to him, convince him that they should use her as bait so they could stop the atrocities on board the *Dorian Rae*. But first she needed to find out what had happened in his past that made him so dead set against letting her help. Why did he blame himself for the deaths of his wife and child?

Vaguely she was aware that he wasn't kissing her back. But she sensed there was something powerful waiting at the gate. A passion that would overwhelm her if unleashed. A passion so controlled and intense that it both frightened and thrilled her. Jess knew she was playing with fire. But the need to reach him was too powerful to resist.

"Something's tearing you apart," she whispered, pulling away just enough to make eye contact. "Talk to me."

"You don't want to know my demons."

"I want to know everything about you."

His gaze searched hers. "Some things are better left alone." He started to pull away. "This is one of them."

"That may be true." She stopped him with her hand on his arm. "But sometimes things only fester if you don't talk about them."

Jess wasn't exactly sure what happened next. One moment he was gazing at her with an intensity that took her breath away. The next his mouth came down on hers so hard she felt his tooth nick her lip. The power of the kiss stunned her. All she could think was that the beast within him had broken free. A beast that had been hurting and alone for a very long time.

Setting his hands on either side of her face, he ravished her mouth with his. Jess kissed him back in kind, but it wasn't enough. She wanted more. When his tongue grazed her lips, seeking entrance, she opened to him. A groan rumbled up from his throat and he went in deep.

His kiss took her breath away, stole her logic, her resistance fleeing out the window with it.

He leaned into the kiss, and when he moved against her, she could feel the hard ridge of his erection against her pelvis. Her vision blurred as all the blood rushed from her brain to erogenous zones she hadn't known existed.

She tried desperately to gather the shattered remains of her composure. But his mouth against hers was like a drug and she couldn't seem to put together more than a passing thought.

He broke the kiss and ran his tongue down her throat to a sensitive place just above her clavicle.

"We...need...to talk...about this," she managed.

"I don't want talk." He punctuated the words by taking her mouth again. "Just this."

Jess gasped in both pleasure and surprise when he cupped her breasts. She'd never seen herself as a sexual person. But the instant his hands made contact, her body began to weep for him. The sensation was maddening and thrilling at once. She groaned when he slipped his hands beneath her sweatshirt. A flick of his wrist and her bra opened. Then the rough skin of his palms met the smooth flesh of her breasts. A cry escaped her when he took her nipples between his thumbs and forefingers and gently squeezed.

Her blood heated and pounded like fists inside her body. She could hear herself breathing hard, like a marathon runner seconds past the finish line.

"Lift your arms."

Jess didn't think. She lifted her arms. As Madrid slid the sweatshirt from her body, her hair cascaded over her shoulders. Before she could gather her wits, he swept her into his arms and carried her to the settee.

It didn't seem big enough for two people. But Jess didn't care. The only thing her mind could focus on at the moment was the magic exploding between them. He laid her on the cushion, then stepped back. She shivered when his dark eyes swept over her, feeling every inch of his perusal like the feather touch of a lover's fingers.

Kneeling, he leaned closer and kissed her. "This is going to change everything."

"I know." Jess jolted when his hands went to the snap of her jeans. Physically, she'd never wanted anything so badly in her life. But on an intellectual level, she knew it was dangerous territory for a woman fresh out of a bad marriage and running for her life. Could she risk her heart on a man who couldn't give her his?

Madrid didn't give her a chance to ponder the

question too long. He worked her jeans over her hips and down her legs, his eyes skimming over her until her body quivered.

"I shouldn't want you," he whispered. "But you take my breath away."

The words touched her. The emotion in his voice devastated her. In his eyes the flash of uncertainty, of vulnerability tore down the last of her defenses. She wanted him on so many levels her mind couldn't begin to sort through them. She wanted to tell him that, but there were no words that could describe the feelings burgeoning in her chest, the passion rising like a flood in her body.

Never taking his eyes from hers, he unfastened his own jeans and tossed them to the floor. Jess had seen men without clothes before; she'd been married for five years. But the sight of Mike Madrid standing before her fully aroused and wearing nothing more than his boxer shorts made her as excited and nervous as a virgin.

"You take my breath away, too," she said.

Surprising her, he laughed. It was a deep, melodic sound that broke some of the tension. His expression softened when he leaned close. "In that case maybe I ought to kiss you before both of us asphyxiate."

Jess laughed, her nerves smoothing out. He joined her and for a precious moment, their laughter rang out like music. When she turned to him, another kind of tension stole through her body. A tension that made her muscles quiver, her body ache with need.

He kissed her hard on the mouth, and her pulse spiked. Every nerve ending in her body quivered when he ran his hands down her sides. Jess had wanted to talk to him before things got this far. She'd wanted to look inside his heart, see if she could find the source of his pain. Help him heal.

But one touch from Madrid and she was too caught up in the moment to think about anything except the heat of his flesh against hers.

Tearing his mouth from hers, he dipped his head and took her nipple into his mouth. He suckled her hard, first one breast and then the other. A groan escaping her, she writhed beneath his ministrations. Vaguely she was aware of him sliding her panties over her hips and down her legs. Suddenly it seemed as if things were moving too quickly. There was too much passion. Too much danger. Not only physical danger, but the kind of danger that could shatter a heart...

Words that would slow things down fluttered

through her mind but died in her throat when he cupped her mound. She opened to him, all thoughts of caution fleeing when he slid two fingers into her and went deep.

Pleasure zinged through her body. Her thought processes shut down. For the span of several seconds all she could focus on was the pleasure. She could feel her body melting around him, her blood heating in her veins. She felt wanton and out of control. The power of those feelings frightened her, but the response was primal and honest and came from somewhere deep inside.

"Let go."

His voice came to her as if from a fog. She opened her eyes to look at him. His expression was taut and his eyes burned into her with intensity. All the while he stroked her toward a kind of madness she hadn't known existed.

The climax rushed over her like an avalanche. Jess felt herself tumbling end over end. Heat burned her from the inside out, her body seeming to explode with it. Madrid spoke softly, but she could no longer understand the words. She didn't try to; she simply let herself feel.

Her body was still in the throes of climax when he moved over her. She opened to him, need coiling and flexing inside her. Dipping his head, he kissed her hard on the mouth, she kissed him back in kind. His tongue entered her at the same time he pushed into her body.

The sensation of being filled by him rent a moan from her throat. Jess threw her head back, and her hips rose to meet his. Bracing his arms on either side of her, he began to move in long, sure strokes that hurled her to the razor's edge a second time.

The intensity of the pleasure overwhelmed her. Finding his mouth with hers, she kissed him deeply, offering everything that made her a woman. And still he moved within her.

A growl rumbled up from his chest. His strokes quickened, his arms began to quiver. Never taking his eyes from hers, Madrid lowered himself onto her more fully and took her face between his hands. Overwhelmed by sensation, by the truth she saw in his eyes, Jess couldn't speak. But at that moment she didn't need words to know what was in his heart.

Lowering his mouth to hers, he spilled his seed into the deepest reaches of her body.

And touched her soul.

Chapter Fifteen

Madrid lay in the darkness and watched the moonlight dance on the wall. Next to him, Jess lay warm and still. It was so quiet he could hear the soft whisper of her breathing. He should have been asleep himself, considering he was working on two days without it. But his mind refused to give him respite.

He'd done the one thing he'd sworn he wouldn't do. He'd let himself get close to Jess. He wanted to believe what had happened between them was about sex. But the physical joy he'd experienced with Jess went far beyond sex. Far beyond anything he'd ever experienced with another human being. She'd touched something deep inside him. A part of him he'd guarded for the past five years. A part of him he'd vowed never to share again.

Yet here he was, physically sated and lying

next to a beautiful woman who had no idea what she was getting into. Little did she know that his touch—his love—was the kiss of death.

Love?

The word echoed inside his head like a killing shot. The thought frightened him more than facing down any killer. It frightened him because he knew what happened to the people he cared for. It was a truth he had accepted five years ago when he'd lost two people he would have given his own life to protect. Now he'd put Jess in the very same position.

How in the name of God had this happened?

"If you frown any harder your head is going to explode."

He actually started at the sound of her voice. Turning slightly, he risked a look at her. She was propped on an elbow, her expression soft and amused. Her face was pale and lovely in the thin light filtering through the window. Her eyes were liquid and dark and moisture glistened on her full lips.

He wanted her. They'd made love twice and already he was hard and aching. He wished he could forget about the past so he could put his arms around her and make love to her until nothing else mattered in the world.

His conscience wouldn't allow it. Besides, he had neither the luxury nor the freedom. Tonight he'd crossed a line he'd sworn he would never cross. Now the time had come for him to pay for his transgression.

"You should be sleeping," he said.

He stiffened slightly when she snuggled against him, closing his eyes against the quick swipe of pleasure. Oh, how he wanted to reach for her and kiss her until they were both mindless with pleasure.

"You're tense."

"Yeah, well, in case you've forgotten there are a few people out there who'd like to see us both dead." He hadn't meant the words to come out so harshly, but she was making him want her and that was ticking him off. What he had done went against everything he believed in.

"Madrid."

He knew what was coming, so he didn't acknowledge her. He didn't even look at her, just continued staring at the ceiling, hoping he had the discipline to do the right thing and stay the hell away from her if she reached for him.

Too late.

"What happened five years ago?" she asked.

Madrid said nothing.

"Don't shut me out."

He did look at her then, drinking in the soft beauty of her face, the determination in her eyes. And he knew no matter how much he wanted her to, she wasn't going to let this go. "I screwed up, Jess. I got two people I cared about killed."

Sympathy scrolled across her features, but she didn't look away. "I'm sorry."

"Yeah. Me, too."

"Why do you blame yourself?"

He sighed, closed his eyes briefly. "Because I'm the one who killed them."

Jess felt the words like a brass-knuckle punch. Until an hour ago she'd had no idea Madrid had been married or that he'd been a father. He'd never spoken of his past. She couldn't imagine the horrific pain of losing both a spouse and a child. Or the agony of blaming himself.

"How did it happen?"

Her instincts told her not to prod. She could plainly see that his pain was like an open wound. But Jess sensed this was something that had been festering inside him for a long time. Something he needed to get out so he could heal and, if he was lucky, move on with his life.

Lacing his hands behind his head, he lay back

on the settee and looked up at the ceiling. "I was a hacker with the CIA back then."

"A hacker?"

"I worked with encryption mostly."

"Sounds fascinating."

"It was boring for the most part, but I was into it. I was cocky." He sighed. "Then along came a terrorist group known as Tiger Eye. The CIA intercepted some encrypted messages. Files sent via e-mail that were encrypted in graphic images. It was my job to find out what they were saying, what they were planning." Another sigh slid from his lips. "This was pre 9/11. Security wasn't as tight as it is now. Even though I was pretty much a peon working behind the scenes, someone inside the agency leaked my name. Someone from Tiger Eye got hold of it. They contacted me, threatened to kill me and my family if I broke their code to the CIA."

"That must have been frightening."

A bitter smile twisted his mouth. "It ticked me off mostly. But I was cocky back then. Too damn cocky. I went to my superior, told her everything. They put my wife and daughter in a protection program and I continued working on breaking the code."

Another sigh slid from his lips. Only this time

Jess thought she heard a quiver. "I got the call at just past three o'clock in the morning. Somehow the terrorists had found out where my family was hiding. Armed terrorists stormed the house in the middle of the night. Two CIA agents were killed and two more were critically wounded."

"And your wife and daughter?"

"Shot execution-style."

The images that forced their way into her head made Jess feel ill. For two innocent lives that were lost. For the grief and loss and guilt that must have fallen like a ton of bricks onto this man's shoulders.

His gaze met hers. Something dark and determined glittered in their depths. "They recorded everything. Sent me the tape." His jaw flexed. "They'd begged for their lives."

His voice broke with the last word, but he quickly regrouped. "I've learned to take threats a hell of a lot more seriously."

Jess didn't have to ask what he was referring to. She knew the loss of his wife and daughter was the reason he wouldn't use her as bait. She couldn't blame him. But it didn't change the situation they were in.

He winced when she reached out and set her palm against his face. "I'm so sorry."

His jaw flexed. "Yeah."

"Were the killers caught?"

"No."

Another piece of the puzzle fell into place. Jess thought she was finally beginning to get a glimpse into the man who'd kept himself so hidden away. The man who drove himself so relentlessly.

"Everyone I've ever cared for has ended up dead," he said in a rough voice.

Her gaze snapped to his. "It wasn't your fault."

"My wife and child weren't the only ones, Jess."

She looked at him. A part of her didn't want to hear what he was going to say next. Another part of her knew she must.

"A year ago a woman I cared for deeply was killed in a car accident. We'd argued. She took off."

"Oh, Madrid." Jess couldn't imagine the grief of losing so much in such a short period of time. She stared at him, aware of hot tears building behind her eyes. For the first time the ferocity with which he'd forbidden her to help him nail the smugglers made sense.

"Don't cry," he whispered.

"What you've been through...it's incredibly sad."

"It is." Wrapping his arms around her, he pulled her close. "If I've learned anything from this, it's that life goes on. But you don't ever take it for granted." He pulled back just enough to make eye contact. "And you never take needless risks."

She gazed back at him, hurting for him, for the hell he'd been through. "Some things are worth risking."

"If you're talking about putting yourself on the line, Jess, I'm not going to let you do it."

That he cared and so readily admitted it made her chest swell. But Jess knew eventually she would have to make a decision. And that in doing so she would probably hurt him all over again.

"I have a confession to make," she said, drawing away.

Madrid glanced at her and raised a brow. "You're not going to shock me, are you?"

She smiled, but it felt forced. "I just want to be honest with you."

"About what?"

"I'm not very good at…you know…this," she blurted.

Madrid nodded, but his expression told her he hadn't a clue what she was getting at. "You want to qualify that?"

"Relationships," she said. "I was married for five years. It ended badly. The divorce was... messy."

"That happens sometimes."

"It was my fault, Madrid. The divorce, I mean. I just wasn't good at...the whole relationship thing. In fact, I pretty much sucked at it."

He set both hands against her cheeks and looked into her eyes. "Maybe *he* wasn't good at it, Jess. Did you ever happen to think of that?"

"I'm impulsive," she said. "I take risks. I do stupid things sometimes without considering other people's feelings. I get angry and say things I don't mean."

He kissed the tip of her nose. "I could be way off base, but it sounds like you might be human."

"I don't want to screw this up." She hadn't meant to say it, but the words came out before she had time to think of the repercussions.

"Let met get this straight," he said. "You're not afraid to face down a bunch of cutthroat smugglers, but when it comes to me you want to turn tail and run?"

"That pretty much covers it." She gave him a self-deprecating smile. "You scare me, Madrid."

"I'm a pussycat."

She laughed. A second later he joined her, and their laughter rang out, the sound of simple human joy.

Madrid sobered. "All I ask is that you stay out of this smuggling thing. Let me handle it."

Because it was one promise she could not make, Jess lifted her mouth to his. When he resisted, she deepened the kiss.

"You don't fight fair," he muttered.

"No," she agreed. "I don't."

Abruptly Madrid puller her against him and kissed her like a man possessed.

He took her to another precipice, higher and more powerful than the first. As Jess tumbled into another wild free fall, she tried hard not to think about what she would have to do come daylight.

MADRID WOKE to the soft chirp of his cell phone. Groggy with sleep, he squinted at the lighted display and put it to his ear. "Madrid."

"Mike…"

The sound of his brother's voice made the hairs at his nape stand on end. "Matt? What's wrong?"

A groan sounded, then his brother's guttural voice said, "They have the boy. I tried to stop them, but…they shot me."

The words sent an electric shock of fear through Madrid. He jumped to his feet, grabbed his jeans off the floor and stepped into them. "How bad are you hurt?"

"I took a bullet in the gut." He groaned. "I'm bleeding like a pig."

"Is there someone there who can help you?"

"Father Tom. He called an ambulance."

Madrid closed his eyes. "When did this happen?"

"A few minutes ago." Another groan. "Mike, these guys are bad news."

Knowing all too well what the smugglers were capable of, Madrid squeezed his eyes closed. "Did they say anything?"

"They wanted Jess, too. Evidently they thought she was here."

"Till the ambulance arrives I want you to get a towel, then lie down and put the towel over the wound."

"Gotcha."

"Hang tight, buddy."

Madrid disconnected and stood there for a moment trying to pull himself together. He couldn't believe the smugglers had found the church. He'd been so careful.

"What happened?"

He spun at Jess's voice, turned to face her. He hated to tell her, but she needed to know. "They have Nicolas."

Her hand went to her mouth. "Oh, God, no."

As he quickly dressed, Madrid related everything his brother had told him. "I have to go."

"I'm going with you."

For the first time since his phone had rung, he gave her his full attention. "No."

"It's me they want."

"And Nicolas."

Sickened by the thought, Jess wrapped herself in a blanket and rose. "I can't sit back and let them hurt that child. I made a promise to Angela."

Madrid spun on her. His hands snaked out, grasped her arms and shook. "I can't let them hurt you!" he roared. "For God's sake, Jess, let me handle this!"

The fury behind his words stopped her; his fingers bit into her skin.

As if realizing he was holding her too tightly, he released her and took a step back. For several interminable seconds they stared at each other. Then Madrid shook himself as if waking from a terrible dream. He pulled a small device from the clip on his belt. "I've only got one weapon and

I need to take it with me." He shoved the device and his cell phone into her hands. "Take these."

"What is this?" she asked, referring to the device.

"GPS. If anything happens, if you feel you're in danger, hit the red button here." He motioned to a small red button on the end of the device. "It's programmed to put out what's called a Code 99. All MIDNIGHT agents will be scrambled. A GPS signal will be activated simultaneously. You got that?"

"I got it."

"Jess, don't open the door for anyone but me. Is that clear?"

"Madrid—"

He cut her off. "If someone comes in through the front, you go out that back window and run for your life. You got that?"

Fear hit home with the words. Until this moment she'd felt safe. Maybe because she was with Madrid.

"I got it," she said.

"Good girl." He lifted his hand as if to touch her cheek, but changed his mind and dropped it. "I have to go."

"Where?"

"The only place I can think of." Giving her a

final, hard look, he snagged his pistol off the counter, flung open the door and was quickly swallowed by darkness.

Chapter Sixteen

In less than five minutes Jess was bouncing off the walls. She couldn't stop thinking about Nicolas. The little boy was in grave danger. The thought of how frightened and confused he must be tore her up inside. The realization that she'd let down her friend was unbearable.

"I'm sorry, Angela," she whispered.

Jess paced the confines of the RV, feeling trapped and helpless and so frustrated she wanted to scream. She thought about Madrid, and frustration transformed quickly into worry. Armed only with a revolver and facing a dozen men armed with semiautomatic weapons, he didn't stand a chance. Would he contact MID-NIGHT for backup? She couldn't think of anyone else he would trust. Even if he did contact someone to watch his back, would they get there in time?

The thought of Madrid getting hurt—or worse—because he was too heroic to involve her tied her into knots. Everything they'd shared in the hours before he left came rushing back. The sadness in his eyes when he spoke of the past. The gentle brush of his touch. The soft whisper of his voice. The heat in his eyes when he looked at her...

The chirp of the cell phone Madrid had left her jerked her from her reverie. A number she didn't recognize came up on the display. "Hello?"

"Jess? It's Father Matthew."

Surprise rippled through her. "Are you all right?" she asked. "Have you heard anything about Nicolas?"

"Unfortunately no. I'm in an ambulance on the way to the hospital." His voice sounded weak and very much like Madrid's. In the background she could hear sirens. "Is Mike still there?" he asked.

"He left five minutes ago."

"Look, it's probably not important, but I thought of something after I hung up."

"What?"

"Well, I've spent quite a bit of time with Nicolas since you and Mike left him here at the church. I have some experience with children who for whatever reason are noncommunicative. When I had dinner with him last night... Well, I know this might sound a little crazy, but I think he's been trying to tell us something."

Jess found herself leaning forward, clutching the phone tightly. "Like what?"

Matt continued. "Early on we thought he was calling out for his mother."

Mah-mah. Mah-mah.

Jess recalled clearly the little boy's wrenching cries. "I remember."

"The more time I spent with him, the more I came to realize he was not calling out for his mother. I think he was repeating a name he'd heard. Maybe even during the crime."

Mah-mah. Mah-mah.

The hair on Jess's nape prickled as realization struck her like a punch. "My God."

"What?"

"Mummert," she whispered. "Chief of Police Mummert."

"You think he's in on it?"

"I think he murdered Angela." Thinking of her friend, she closed her eyes. "I have to go."

"Jess—"

Knowing he would try to talk her out of what she was about to do, Jess disconnected. For a moment she gripped the cell phone, her mind reeling. Angela had believed Mummert to be an ally. Had she confided in Mummert? Had she told him about the MIDNIGHT Agency and her investigation? Did he know Madrid was a MIDNIGHT Agent?

The thought of Madrid walking into a trap made her knees go weak. She looked down at the cell phone. He'd given her his only means of communication; there was no way to call him, warn him. He'd told her to stay put. But how could she when he could be walking into an ambush?

She couldn't stay here and do nothing while the man she loved walked into a trap. But Madrid had left her without a vehicle. The shipyard was too far away to reach on foot. She could call a cab, but that would entail a wait and involve another person. She could try to find a vehicle with the keys left in the ignition.

It dawned on her then that she could drive the RV.

Dashing to the front of the vehicle, she shoved open the door to the cab. She got an impression of bucket seats with a console in the center. Large steering wheel. Digital dash. No keys.

Where are the keys?

Then she remembered seeing Madrid take

the keys from a cabinet, and dashed into the galley. She flung open the cabinet door and her heart stuttered when she spotted a single key dangling from a hook.

"I'm sorry, Madrid," she whispered as she darted back to the cab and climbed into the driver's seat. "But there's no way in hell I'm going to let you get yourself killed."

JESS PARKED the RV on the same muddy road she and Madrid had used the night before. As soon as she was on board the ship, she would call Jake Vanderpol and let him know what she was doing in case something went wrong.

It took her ten minutes to find the opening Madrid had cut in the chain-link fence. Evidently no one from the shipyard had discovered it. The place wasn't exactly bustling, but still, in a post-9/11 world it surprised her that the port police were not more careful with security.

Silently Jess ducked through the hole. Sticking to the shadows, she sprinted toward the docks. All the while her mind conjured visions of armed smugglers and cops on the take, and she found herself wondering how she was going to stop them when all she had was a cell phone and a flashlight. Not exactly an arsenal. Then she reminded herself that these ruthless men had Nicolas, and she realized she didn't have a choice but to try. If she could find Madrid, she could tell him what she knew about Mummert, and maybe between the two of them and Jake Vanderpol they could come up with a plan and stop these bastards once and for all.

Her boots clicked quietly against the asphalt as she jogged down the concrete pier toward the *Dorian Rae*. Around her, the other ships moved restlessly against their moorings, the ropes groaning like bound ghosts. As she neared the *Dorian Rae,* she spotted the gangplank, a stairway that led to the bulwark on the quarterdeck. Last time she had been here, it hadn't been there. Farther down the dock, a forklift carrying a box on pallets started toward her.

Realizing they were in the process of loading the ship, Jess took the gangplank at a run. The black water thirty feet below seemed to mock her as she made her way to the bulwark. Remembering the cold grip of it, she shivered and hurried ahead.

On the quarterdeck she paused and looked around. There was no one in sight, but she knew there were people on board. Somewhere in the distance a diesel engine rumbled. To her right a rat scampered along a rope as thick as a man's arm. On the deck above her, she could hear voices.

She needed a plan. But outnumbered and out-manned as she was, an effective strategy wasn't going to be easy to come up with. She wondered if Nicolas was on board. A shudder went through her when she thought of all the terrible things that could happen to the little boy at sea.

At the sound of footsteps her head jerked up. Silhouetted against the lights of the bridge to her right, she saw two men walking toward her. Jess's heart leaped into a sprint. Looking around wildly, she hopped over a rope rail, then ducked into an alcove.

The men stopped less than ten feet away. If she moved one inch in the wrong direction, she thought, the men would see her. Pressing her back against the wall, Jess tried to make herself as flat as possible and prayed they didn't get any closer.

A full minute passed. Craning her neck slightly, she peered around a steel beam. The men, smoking cigarettes, were both dressed in dark slacks and company jackets. Leaning against the rail beside them were nasty-looking automatic rifles. Lovely.

"We should be under way within the hour." One of the men spoke with an accent.

"I'll feel a hell of a lot better once we're out to sea." The second man slid a flask from his jacket pocket, took a long pull, then passed it to his companion. "The last thing we need right now is problems because of Mummert's screwup."

"In another hour we'll be in international waters. Once there, we're home free." He jabbed a thumb in the direction of a small airtight hatch directly to his left. "We might even get to sample some of our cargo, if you know what I mean."

"I'm in this for the money," the second man said, "not the fringe benefits."

"Pretty self-righteous for a smuggler."

"Yeah, well, I don't like the idea of offing that kid."

"Think of the alternative and you'll come to terms." Leaning over, the first man picked up his rifle.

The second man shoved the flask into his jacket and picked up his own weapon. "Let's finish our security sweep and get below deck. I'm getting cold and there's a card game heating up in the mess hall."

Jess stood with her back pressed against the wall for a full minute after the men were out of sight. When she trusted her legs to move, she stepped out of the alcove, her head reeling.

I don't like the idea of offing that kid.

Think of the alternative and you'll come to terms.

She knew in her heart they were talking about Nicolas. What she didn't understand was how two human beings could accept something so monstrous as killing an innocent child. The thought brought tears to her eyes.

But Jess didn't let herself cry. There was no time. The *Dorian Rae* was about to head out to sea. And she had to find Nicolas before the ship left port.

She glanced at the hatch the man had motioned to. A shiver swept through her at the thought of sneaking below deck again. She and Madrid had seen where the women were being held captive. She'd seen the blood, the shackles.

We might even get to sample some of our cargo, if you know what I mean.

The man's words drifted through her mind. Were they talking about human cargo? Did they have women on board now? Until this moment Jess had been under the impression that they were smuggling illegal immigrants into the United States. But smuggling women out of the country, as well? Who were the women? Runaways? And where were these men taking them?

The whole scenario sickened her.

Taking a fortifying breath, she twisted the wheel lock, pulled open the hatch and stepped into the semidarkness. The hatch closed with a resounding click behind her. Around her, steel pipes clanged and pinged, the ceiling creaked. Claustrophobia threatened, but Jess staved it off by sheer will. She couldn't turn back now. Nicolas was relying on her.

Slowly, cautiously she moved down the narrow corridor, her shoes nearly silent on the steel floor. Twenty feet into the hall, she came upon another hatch. Setting her hands on the wheel, she turned it twice and the hatch hissed open. She went through it and another corridor stretched out before her. The odors of mildew, oily water and something else dark and earthy filled her nostrils. Jess squinted into the near darkness, but the corridor was empty. Pulling the flashlight from her waistband, she flicked it on. The beam illuminated steel walls stained red with rust and dripping with condensation.

She thought she and Madrid had taken this same route the night before, but nothing looked familiar. As she made her way down the narrow corridor, she desperately wished for a blueprint of the ship. Nicolas could be anywhere and she had no idea where to look.

The sound of steel against steel sent her heart into her throat. Gasping, Jess spun, brought up the flashlight. Terror slammed into her at the sight of the two men crowded into the doorway and holding ugly-looking rifles trained on her chest.

"Well, well, well, what do we have here?"

Chapter Seventeen

Jess's pulse raced out of control as a tall man
with a scraggly beard looked her up and down.
They were the same two men she'd encountered
on deck. The men who'd been so nonchalantly
discussing the murder of an innocent child.

"Looks like we got us a stowaway," said the
man.

His partner nodded. "A ship is a dangerous
place. Anything could happen to a stowaway
and no one would ever know."

Jess's heart was pounding so hard she could
barely hear the words. But she didn't need to
hear their voices to know they wouldn't think
twice about harming her.

"I—I must have taken a wrong turn." A dumb
response, but it was the only explanation she
could think of with her heart doing acrobatics
in her chest and her mind spinning like a top.

The bearded man lunged at her. She felt the scrape of his fingertips against her arm and danced back. Simultaneously she brought up the flashlight, hoping the beam would temporarily blind him. A curse burned through the air, and she caught a glimpse of his lips pulled back into a snarl, his eyes glinting with savage intent. And all she could think was that they were going to kill her and no one would ever know.

If anything happens...hit the red button.

Madrid's words flashed through her mind. She stumbled back. Her hand went to the device clipped to her belt. She fumbled with it till her fingers found the button and pressed it.

An instant later the flashlight was knocked from her hand. Vaguely she was aware of it skittering away. Screaming, Jess spun and threw herself into a run, the footsteps behind her spurring her faster. She was midway to the hatch when two strong arms grabbed her shoulders and spun her around.

"Where do you think you're going?"

She lashed out with her fists, but the man was strong and fast and overpowered her with ease. Jess fought him, but she was no match. Shoving her face-first into the wall hard enough to bruise her cheek, he jerked her hands behind her back.

"Give me the rope," he snapped to his partner.

Jess tried to jerk her hands free, but her efforts were in vain. She closed her eyes as the man tied her wrists.

Roughly the man spun her around to face them. She cringed when his gaze swept over her, lingering on her breasts. "Who are you and what are you doing here?" he demanded.

"I—I told you," Jess said in a shaking voice. "I must have taken a wrong turn."

The two men exchanged looks. "So what do we do with her?" the other guy asked. "Throw her in the brig with the others?"

The bearded man sneered. "She ain't lost. I'd lay odds this bitch is Customs." He all but snarled at her. "Or a damn cop."

"A cop?" The second man looked alarmed. "I don't want no part of this if she's a cop. I'm on parole."

"That won't matter." Her captor lifted his hand to her face, ran his finger down her cheek and smiled. "Unless she can swim with an anchor around her neck."

MADRID STARED at the blueprints spread out on the table, putting every level, every hatch, every corridor to memory. Next to him, Jake Vander-pol shoved hollow-point rounds into a clip.

"I'd lay odds he's on the ship," Madrid said.

Jake jammed the full clip into the Beretta and shoved the pistol into his shoulder holster. "If there wasn't so much steel, we could get infrared."

"No time for that."

"Yeah." Jake grimaced. "So are we going in after him or what?"

Both men jumped when Jake's cell phone chirped. Madrid knew what the display would read even before Jake showed it to him.

Code 99.

Jess.

Jake hit the retrieve button for the text message details. *Madrid. Code 99. All available agents respond. Waypoint: N3801.650 W12257.754.*

"That's your code, partner."

Jake's voice came to him as if out of a fog. Madrid's gaze snapped to him. "I gave my GPS unit to Jess."

"Looks like she's in trouble."

Jake was studying him closely, as if expecting him to explode at any moment. "I told her to stay put."

"Has there ever been any time in your life when a woman has done what you've asked?"

Madrid barely heard the words. "I have to go."

"Not alone you don't."

"Cutter isn't going to condone this."

"He doesn't condone half of what we do." Jake looked down at the coordinates and punched numbers into a larger GPS hand-held unit. His brows snapped together. "Looking at the grid, I'd say she's on board the ship, partner."

Nausea rose inside Madrid at the thought of Jess being on board the *Dorian Rae* alone and at the hands of brutal smugglers. "I think that's where the boy is, too."

Jake Vanderpol started for the door. "Let's bring them home."

JESS COULDN'T BELIEVE she'd screwed up so royally. What was she thinking, rushing into a potentially dangerous situation without a plan and without someone to back her up? But she knew where her mind had been. She'd been thinking of a five-year-old boy with special needs. A child who'd already been through so much and was once again facing terrible danger.

A hand between her shoulder blades shoved her forward. She stumbled, wondering if Madrid had gotten her message. If he knew she was in trouble. If he would be able to reach her in time to save her and Nicolas.

They came to another corridor and went left, up some steel stairs and through another hatch. The corridor here was wider and better lit. Beyond, she heard voices. At the end of the hall, light spilled from a doorway. Dread and a new terror rose inside her when she realized they were probably taking her to whoever was in charge to decide what to do with her. It didn't take much imagination to figure out what that fate might be.

She paused outside the door, her heart pounding. She didn't want to go inside. She didn't want to face those men. She considered trying to break free and making a run for it.

"Move it." A rough hand shoved her through the portal. Jess stumbled into a room filled with cigarette smoke. Half a dozen male faces jerked in her direction. Six unshaven men sat at a table with cards and money spread out before them.

"Ah, Jessica Atwood. What a pleasant and unexpected surprise."

The familiarity of the voice jolted her. Jess scanned the room, her gaze landing on the source. Norm Mummert. Even though she'd suspected his involvement in the smuggling ring, the sight of the police chief still stunned her. Up until yesterday he'd represented the good guys.

"I'm glad you could join us," he said.

"I can't say the same." She tried to make her voice come out strongly, but the words were little more than a squeak.

She looked around the room, shuddering inwardly at the expressions of the men staring back. She turned her eyes to Mummert. "I can't believe you're part of this," she said.

He shrugged amicably. "We do what we must."

"And what is that?" she asked, unable to keep the rancor from her voice. "Kill innocent children?"

"Unfortunately, collateral damage is part of the cost of doing business in this industry. You understand."

"What I understand is that you murdered one of your own in cold blood."

"Interesting you should mention Angela. I'd like to hear all about her. I understand she was working undercover. Some kind of federal agent." He tsked. "Her death was an unfortunate complication. I liked her very much. Good thing we had you to take the fall, wasn't it?"

"She trusted you, you son of a bitch."

Twisted amusement danced in his eyes. "She

always was too trusting." The amusement turned cruel and hard. "My only true regret is the boy. But then that brings us back to our real lack of options here, doesn't it?"

Jess choked back a sob at the thought of Nicolas being hurt. "He's a defenseless child."

"He saw too much and now he's in the way."

She looked around, half expecting to see the child tied to a chair. "Where is he?"

"In a safe place."

"I want to see him."

"You're in no position to be making demands."

Jess envisioned herself launching herself at him, clawing at his face and eyes and neck with her nails. She wanted to hurt him. She wanted to stop him before he did something irrevocable.

"He's just a little boy," she pleaded. "Please, let him go. He can't speak."

"I'm afraid I can't take that risk. You see, both of you are witnesses to something I do not want coming to light."

"You mean your human smuggling operation?"

Something dark and unsettling glinted in his eyes. "You get an A-plus for ingenuity. It's unfortunate that both of you will have to die for it.

It won't take much to make the police believe you killed Angela, took her son and fled the country."

"They'll never believe it."

"You have…shall we say, a history of running away from problems."

"Mike Madrid knows the truth." The words were out before she could stop them. She knew better than to speak of Madrid, but she was desperate and terrified and grasping at straws.

"Ah, I see. You and the federal agent have grown close."

"No." She panted the word, breathless with fear and panic. "He knows all about your operation."

Mummert stood abruptly. Jess shrank away from him when he approached her. Gripping her chin with his hand, he squeezed hard enough to cause pain and forced her gaze to his. "You have no idea how many problems you've caused me."

"Your problems are just beginning." She ground out the words.

An evil smile split his face. "I will take no pleasure in hurting that child. But I'm going to enjoy seeing you die."

Jess responded the only way she could and spat in his face.

Mummert's cheeks reddened. She barely had time to brace when he struck her with an open-handed slap hard enough to snap her teeth together. Pain zinged from cheekbone to jaw, fierce enough to make her eyes water.

Stepping back, he shook himself, then turned his attention to one of the other men. "Prepare the *Dorian Rae* for departure. I want to be out of this port by oh four hundred." He glanced at his watch. "I want to be in international waters before dawn so I can watch this little bitch die."

He looked at Jess. "Take her to the brig and secure an anchor around her neck."

Jess stared at him, shock and horror punching her. "No!" she screamed. "You can't do this."

"I can, and I will." He nodded to the two men holding her arms. "Go," he said to them.

Jess fought them with all her might, but with her hands bound behind her she was helpless. "Please!" she cried. "At least let the little boy go. Please!"

Mummert gave her that evil smile again. "You should have thought of him before you got involved in this, princess."

Chapter Eighteen

Madrid had been in plenty of iffy situations in the years he'd been with the MIDNIGHT Agency. He'd been scared out of his wits too many times to count. But for the life of him he couldn't remember a time when the fear had been quite so paralyzing. The kind of cold terror that permeated all the way to his bones.

It was a cruel twist that the fear was not born of self-preservation, but the safety of someone he loved.

The realization that he'd fallen in love with Jess stunned him. Made him realize she meant the world to him. That he would do any-thing—including risk his own life—to save her and Nicolas.

If only he knew how.

"You got it bad for her, huh, Madrid?"

Jake Vanderpol's voice jerked him from his

reverie. For a moment he just stared at the other man, not sure how to answer without changing the dynamics of the situation. But in the end he decided on the truth. "Worse than bad."

They were in Vanderpol's car heading toward Humboldt Bay. Madrid motioned right and they turned onto the same dirt road he and Jess had used the night before. His heart jigged in his chest when he spotted the RV. "She's here."

The car fishtailed in mud when Vanderpol hit the brakes.

"Could be a trap," he suggested.

But Madrid already had the door open. He hit the ground running, praying he would find her inside the RV. In the far distance he heard Vanderpol shout his name, but he didn't stop. He had both his gun and flashlight out, a bullet chambered by the time he reached the RV. He burst into the vehicle and did a quick sweep of the place, but she wasn't there. But then he'd known he would find the place empty. He'd been hoping for a miracle.

He jolted when Vanderpol came up behind him and set his hand on his shoulder. "She's on board the ship, partner."

Cursing beneath his breath, Madrid went to

the car, to the satchel of items he'd taken from Angela's house.

"What are you doing?" Vanderpol asked.

"Hoping to find a tool that will help us get on board the ship."

Vanderpol looked at the bag. "Angela's?"

"Yeah." Madrid pulled out a small device that looked like a crossbow that had been equipped with some type of reel.

Vanderpol grinned. "She always was into gadgets."

"Good thing, because this one is probably going to save her son's life."

JESS COULD NEVER have imagined her life ending this way. With so much left undone. With so much love in her heart. She thought of Madrid, and hot tears burned her eyes.

"Keep walking, bitch."

The words were punctuated by a hard shove. Fury and a cold, numbing fear permeated her as two men forced her down the narrow corridor. Her mind spun between Madrid and Nicolas. Was Madrid looking for them? If so, would he reach them in time to save their lives?

They stopped at a narrow hatch. One of the men twisted the wheel lock and the door hissed open. Another hard shove forced her through the hatch and sent her to her knees. Before she could struggle to her feet, the hatch slammed with a finality that sent a cold spear of fear right through her center.

Sobbing in frustration, Jess struggled to her feet and looked around. Surprise jolted her when she saw two small faces watching her. A petite Asian woman wearing a torn blue dress and a bruise high on her cheekbone set her hand protectively on Nicolas's shoulder and stepped back.

Jess choked back a sob when she looked at Nicolas. He was wearing the same sweatshirt and jeans he'd worn when she'd left him with Father Matthew and his face was streaked with dirt. But she saw recognition in his eyes. "Nicolas," she cried. "Oh, honey, I'm so glad you're okay."

She went to the boy and fell to her knees, pressing her face to his. She wanted desperately to hold him, but with her hands bound she could not. At the moment, though, it was enough to feel him warm and alive against her.

A full minute passed before she got a handle on her emotions. Pulling away from the boy, she looked at the woman. She saw the fear and mistrust in her eyes, and Jess realized the woman was every bit as frightened as she was. "I'm not going to hurt you," Jess said.

The woman's eyes narrowed, but she didn't speak.

Giving Nicolas a kiss on his cheek, Jess rose to her full height and took a fortifying breath. "I'm glad he's not alone."

"He's very frightened."

Jess nodded, fighting tears. "Who are you?" she asked.

"Chin Lee."

"I'm Jess."

The woman nodded.

"Chin Lee, do you think you could untie me?"

Fear entered the woman's eyes and she shook her head. "It will only anger him."

"Who? Mummert? Someone higher on the food chain?"

Chin Lee averted her eyes, looked down at her small hands.

"Please," Jess pressed. "We've got to get out of here."

"There is no way out."

"Help is on the way," she said. "Federal agents. But we're in danger here. We need to get out now."

Indecision and something that might have

been hope glimmered in the woman's eyes. "The men," she whispered. "They will return soon."

"Please," Jess pleaded. "Quickly. Untie me so I can help you."

The woman bit her lip. Jess didn't look away. They didn't have much time. She could hear the rumble of the engines as the crew prepared the ship for departure. "They're going to kill us," she said. "They're going to kill this child. We have to get out of here now."

The woman nodded. "I will help you."

Jess turned and offered her bound hands. Seconds ticked by like an eternity as the woman worked at the knot. Jess couldn't look, keeping her eyes on the door instead. When she felt the rope fall away, relief swept through her.

"Thank you," she said.

The woman nodded. "You can get us out of here?"

"I'm going to try." First Jess went to Nicolas and hugged him tightly. The boy didn't hug her back, but she could feel his little body relax against hers, and she knew that even though he had gone into his own world, he knew she was there. For now, that was enough.

"He's special," Chin Lee said.

Jess thought of how Nicolas had named his

mother's killer from the very start and she choked out a sound that was part laugh, part sob. "He's a little hero." For the first time she noticed the dirty and well-used toy at his side and another wave of emotion swamped her. Even in this hellhole, this woman had somehow found a small comfort for the little boy.

"It was all I could give him," Chin Lee said.

Blinking back tears, Jess smiled. "It's enough."

Rubbing the rope burns at her wrists, Jess went to the door and tried the handle, found it locked. She looked around the small room. Seeing no windows, no other doors, she was swamped by the sensation of being trapped. A fold-up cot with a thin mattress and threadbare blanket sat in the corner, a plate holding a few crumbs beneath it. A tiny black-and-white television sat on a rickety-looking stool next to the bed.

Jess looked at Chin Lee. "Is there any way out of here?"

"No way out."

She studied the other woman. She was young, but thin and gaunt. "How long have you been here?"

"Two months."

Jess couldn't imagine being held captive

that long in these conditions. "How did you end up here?"

"The man promise me citizenship in the United States."

"Who?"

"Mummert."

Jess chose her next words carefully. "Are there other women on board?"

Chin Lee dropped her eyes, nodded.

"How many?"

"I'm not sure. Fifteen or twenty. Women and girls mostly."

"Where?"

"The brig. One level down. I take them food sometimes."

A dozen questions swirled in Jess's head, but there was no time to talk. If they wanted to live, they were going to have to find a way out.

"Chin Lee, is there a guard outside the door?"

The other woman hesitated, then shook her head. Jess got the feeling there might be a way, but Chin Lee didn't want to talk about it. "They're going to kill us if we don't get out of here," she said.

Chin Lee's eyes were ancient when they met Jess's. "The guard...sometimes he come in here at night." She averted her eyes.

Jess's heart twisted at the thought of the ordeals this poor woman had been forced to endure. "I'm sorry."

Chin Lee's eyes filled with tears.

Sympathy and newfound anger flashed inside Jess. But the part of her that was a survivor was already jumping ahead to ways they could use the situation to their advantage. She looked around the room for anything they could use as a weapon, her eyes settling on the television.

"Is there any way you can get the guard's attention?" she asked. "Maybe call him into the room?"

Chin Lee's eyes widened and she shook her head violently. "No."

"Knock on the door. Tell him you're sick."

"Please, don't. You will be sorry."

"I won't let him hurt you. I promise."

"You can't stop him. He's armed and strong."

"Yeah, well, so are we." Jess walked over to the small television and picked it up, tested its weight. "Here's what we're going to do," she said, and began to outline her plan.

MADRID COULD HEAR the big diesel engines rumbling as he and Vanderpol sprinted along the dock. He didn't have to see the smoke billowing from the dual stacks to know that the big container ship was starting to pull away.

"Where the hell are they going?" Jake muttered.

"My guess is they bring the women here and hide them while money changes hands. Then they unload at Luna Bay under the protection of the Lighthouse Point PD." Madrid shook his head in disgust. "We've got about a minute to get on board that ship."

"Not going to happen," Vanderpol said.

"The hell it's not." Digging into the satchel, Madrid pulled out a length of rope equipped with a four-prong hook.

"What the hell are you doing, man?"

"Saving the lives of two people I care about." Madrid quickly coiled the rope. Setting his hand a foot from the base of the hook, he began to swing it like a lasso. "Are you in or not?"

Jake shook his head. "It's probably going to get me killed, but I'm in."

Madrid tossed the hook. Sweat broke out on the back of his neck when the rope fell short of the departing ship. Cursing, he quickly reeled it in and tried again. This time the hook caught the lowest rung of the rail just above the anchor hawsehole.

"Gotcha!" Madrid whispered.

But the small victory was short-lived. The ship was picking up speed, the engines gunning as the mammoth vessel was maneuvered away from the dock. Madrid felt the rope run through his hands. There was no time to coordinate with Vanderpol. Giving his fellow agent a final look, he grasped the rope with both hands and launched himself off the dock.

"Madrid! *Damn it.*"

His name being called was the last thing he heard before the water rushed up and slammed into him.

JESS STAGED THE SCENE as best she could. Her hands were shaking so badly when she picked up the TV, she wasn't sure she could lift it over her head. She slid the stool behind the door and stepped onto it. Chin Lee had unbuttoned the top two buttons of her dress. Nicolas sat on the bed, rocking back and forth. Next to him, Chin Lee had formed the pillow to look like a female silhouette and draped it with the blanket. Hopefully, the guard would be so distracted by Chin Lee's cleavage that he wouldn't notice it wasn't Jess on the cot.

"Ready?" Chin Lee asked.

Jess nodded. "Do it."

Pursing her lips, Chin Lee pounded on the door. "Help us, please," she cried. "The woman is sick!"

Jess's arms quivered with the weight of the television as she lifted it above her head. Chin Lee pounded the door a second time. "Please, help me!"

Every nerve in Jess's body went taut when the latch clicked. She held her breath as the door swung open. Looking down, she saw the back of a bald head and shoulders as wide as a football field. "Whaddya want?" he asked with a gruff British accent.

Maintaining the guise with the flair of a dramatic actress, Chin Lee pointed to the bed. "She's sick. Not breathing. Need doctor."

"Oh, bloody hell." The man entered the room. "What's wrong with her?"

He must have sensed Jess above him, because he started to turn. But he wasn't fast enough. She brought the television down on his head as hard as she could. The sound of glass breaking shattered the silence of the room. The momentum made Jess lose her balance and she fell forward, crashing into the guard. Vaguely she was aware of him bellowing. Of Nicolas crying. Of Chin Lee rushing toward them.

Jess and the guard hit the floor with a crash. Adrenaline and the promise of escape had Jess on her feet in a fraction of a second. She looked wildly around. Chin Lee stood outside the door in the corridor, keeping watch. Nicolas sat on the bed, whimpering. The guard lay on his back. His eyes were closed; he wasn't moving.

Jess rushed to Nicolas and put her arms around him. "It's going to be okay, sweetie." Hugging him to her, she stroked the back of his head and cooed, "But we have to go, okay?"

The guard groaned. She'd hoped to knock him unconscious, but he was starting to thrash. Her gaze snapped to Chin Lee's. "We need to tie him up."

Chin Lee darted back into the room and gathered the rope that had been used to tie Jess. Working in unison, the two women tied the guard's hands behind his back. When that was finished, Jess confiscated his radio and pistol, shoved both into the waistband of her slacks.

"Let's go." Crossing to Nicolas, Jess lifted him from the cot and took him into her arms. At five years of age, he wasn't exactly light, but she thought she could carry him for a small distance.

"Where?" In the corridor, Chin Lee looked both ways.

"Lifeboats." Meeting her, Jess set Nicolas on his feet and took his hand. "Do you know the way?"

Chin Lee motioned right. "Follow me."

She took off at a jog, Jess trailing with Nicolas in tow. If her memory served her, they were two levels down. Once they reached the deck, Jess thought, even if they couldn't find the lifeboat in time, she would rather risk jumping overboard than face the crew.

They reached a hatch. Two spins and Chin Lee went through it. Their shoes clanged against steel-grate stairs. Nicolas whimpered softly, but Jess encouraged him, hoping the fear leaping through her veins didn't leach into her voice. "Come on, sweetie," she whispered. "You can do it. Just a little farther."

They hit a stairwell, passed a second hatch and continued up. Midway to the final hatch, the blare of an alarm split the air.

"What's that?" Jess asked.

Chin Lee had gone white. "They know," she said. "Hurry."

When they reached the top stairwell, Chin Lee went to work on the door. Jess knelt beside Nicolas and gave him a hug. "We're almost there," she whispered.

The hatch opened. Chin Lee burst through. Taking Nicolas's hand, Jess followed.

And found herself face-to-face with two uniformed men, their semiautomatic weapons trained on her heart.

Chapter Nineteen

The *Dorian Rae* was midway to the mouth of the port by the time Madrid climbed over the rail on the lowest weather deck. The first thing he noticed was the intermittent blast of the alarm.

He was soaked to the skin, but he barely felt the cold as he sprinted along the rail toward the bridge. He'd hated leaving Vanderpol behind— he needed the backup—but Madrid had had a split second to make his decision; he'd done the only thing he could. He had to find Jess and Nicolas. Once the ship reached international waters, he'd never see them again.

Ahead, he saw the bridge lights and the silhouette of the radar mast against the night sky. The ship was massive, and he had no idea where to look for Jess. If he could reach the bridge, maybe he could get the ship stopped.

Ten feet from the deckhouse four men

dressed in uniforms and armed with semiautomatic weapons clattered down a steel stairway. By ducking into a darkened alcove Madrid barely avoided being spotted. He watched them pass, his heart pounding. The men were going somewhere in a hurry. He listened to the scream of the alarm and wondered if it had anything to do with Jess.

Sticking to the shadows, Madrid followed the men. He tried to catch what they were saying, thought he heard the words *security breach*, but he was too far away to be sure. They took him past the wheelhouse, up a short flight of stairs. Ahead, he heard more voices. Drawing his weapon, he slinked up the steps, in plain sight if any of the men had had a notion to turn around. In the near distance he saw the silhouettes of two large lifeboats suspended by ropes and massive pulleys.

His heart stopped in his chest when he spotted them. Two women and a child. *Jess.* Her silhouette was unmistakable. He could tell by her body language that she was frightened. Yet she kept herself squarely between the gunmen and Nicolas.

The need to protect what was his slammed through him. But Madrid had enough experience to know better than to rush into a situation where he was outmanned and outgunned eight to one. Recklessness was the fastest way to getting killed.

He looked down at his weapon and silently cursed its inadequacy. He had a knife strapped to his belt, too. But not even the combination of the two would be enough to stop eight armed men desperate enough to murder women and children. He thought of Vanderpol and wondered if the other man had made it on board.

The only way Madrid was going to get to Jess was if he could come up with some kind of distraction. But for the life of him he couldn't think of a way to stop what he knew would happen next.

His worst nightmare became a reality when he saw the familiar silhouette of a man who was stepping toward Jess. Mummert. Horror flashed inside him when Mummert raised a pistol and leveled it at her. The people he'd loved and lost in his life flashed in his mind's eye. He couldn't believe fate would steal another.

"You've become quite a thorn in my side," Mummert said.

"Go to hell."

If he hadn't been so terrified, Madrid might

have smiled at Jess's response. But while her words were strong, he heard the quiver of terror in her voice.

Mummert ran the muzzle of the pistol from her cheek to her breast. "Though I'm sure you would have made our voyage much more interesting, I'm afraid I have no more time for delays."

In one smooth motion he grasped Nicolas's arm. Jess launched herself at him, but two men moved quickly forward and forced her back.

"Let him go!" she screamed. "He's just a little boy."

Easy, Madrid thought. *Don't push him too hard.*

"Ah, but children make for excellent leverage." Mummert set the pistol against the boy's temple. "Don't you agree?"

"What do you want?" Jess screamed.

He gave her an evil smile. "I want you to jump overboard." He pulled back the slide on the gun. "Or I'll kill him where he stands."

JESS COULDN'T BELIEVE it had come to this. She was standing on the lifeboat platform. Twenty feet down, the ocean taunted her with three-foot whitecaps and the promise of a cold and terrible death.

"Do it," Mummert said.

Terror twisted inside her like barbed wire. Her body screamed with tension as she weighed her options. But there were none. If she refused, Mummert would kill Nicolas. If she jumped, she might live long enough to hear the bullets that would end Chin Lee's and Nicolas's lives. An unfathomable dilemma...

"I'll do it," she said after a moment.

"Of course you will."

"On one condition."

Every nerve in her body jumped when he fired a shot. The hot zing of the bullet whizzed by inches from her ear.

"Stop wasting time," he said.

"Let the boy go. Do what you like with me." Despite her best efforts, a sob squeezed from her throat. "I'll do anything."

"Tempting." Mummert's gaze raked over her. "You certainly have your charms. But the time for play is over. Your time is up. So is the boy's. Now, jump or I'll put a bullet in his head."

Jess stood facing them with the water to her back. Eight men, all of them willing to murder an innocent child for the likes of whatever money their illegal cargo would bring them once they reached their destination.

In the back of her mind she wondered if Madrid had gotten her message. If he was trying to reach her. Considering she had mere minutes left, she accepted the reality that he wasn't going to arrive in time.

"You coldhearted bastard," she choked.

Mummert gave her an odd half smile. "That would be true if I had a heart. Make no mistake, my beauty—I do not." He shifted the gun to Nicolas again.

"Don't," she pleaded.

"Jump or I'll make sure you see him die."

Jess wanted to take at least one of them with her. For a crazy instant she considered charging Mummert, tackling him, taking him over the side and into the water. But she knew he would shoot her down before she got close enough.

Her only consolation was that her hands weren't bound. She would be able to swim. But judging by the lights back at the shipyard, the vessel was already half a mile out. She would succumb to hypothermia long before she reached the shore.

She looked at Nicolas and couldn't hold back the rush of tears. "Everything's going to be okay," she choked.

It was a lie. They were going to die.

She hadn't wanted to give Mummert the satisfaction of seeing her break down. But the injustice was too great. The heartbreak of an innocent child's impending death shattered her.

Giving Nicolas a final look, she turned her back to them and faced the sea. She thought of Madrid, and another layer of grief fell over her. She loved him with all her heart. He was the kind of man she would have been able to spend the rest of her life with. Why hadn't she recognized that when she'd been with him?

Terror stole through her when she looked down at the black, churning water. Her entire body shook violently when she stepped toward the edge of the platform.

"I love you, Madrid," she whispered. "Always."

Closing her eyes, she stepped closer to the edge of the platform. Behind her she heard Mummert shout something, but Jess's heart was pounding too hard for her to hear. She visualized herself jumping, her body slamming into the cold water, the black abyss sucking her down.

Her foot reached the edge of the platform. Terror raged like a wild beast inside her. A scream waited to burst from her throat. *Oh, dear God, help me.*

The platform jolted violently beneath her

feet, throwing her off balance. She dropped to her knees as a bullet whizzed over her head. She heard shouts from the ship and looked over her shoulder to see one of the huge lifeboats plummet into the crowd of men. The uninjured men scattered, and Jess caught a glimpse of Chin Lee grabbing Nicolas. When a second lifeboat plunged into the water, Jess looked up to see a huge plume of fire and smoke billow from the aft stack.

"The engine room!" someone yelled.

Out of the chaos, a black-clad figure swung down from one of the lifeboat pulleys. Hope burst inside Jess when she realized it was Madrid.

She screamed his name on the wind. In her peripheral vision she saw him gather Nicolas into his arms. With Chin Lee behind him, he hit the platform at a sprint.

His eyes met Jess's. "Jump!" he shouted. *"Jump!"*

He didn't give her a chance to hesitate. Snagging her hand in his, he hauled her over the side of the platform. Time stood still as they free-fell. Vaguely she was aware of shots being fired behind them.

Then the water rushed up and slammed into her like a solid block of ice. The cold snatched the breath from her lungs, and the water enveloped her like icy hands, shook her, tumbled her.

But Madrid never let go of her hand. His warmth was like a lifeline, the only thing that separated life from death. She kicked, hoping the buoyancy of her body would float her to the top quickly.

An instant later Jess broke the surface. Next to her she saw the white oval of Madrid's face. He was holding Nicolas. The little boy was crying and struggling, but he was alive. It was the most beautiful sight Jess had ever seen.

"Get in the lifeboat!" Madrid shouted.

Treading water, Jess looked around, spotted the small craft twenty feet away. Another layer of relief swept through her when she spotted Chin Lee already hanging on to the side.

Jess didn't know how she made it to the boat. Using the last of her strength, she clung to the side. Then strong arms were pulling her on board. She looked up to see Madrid's eyes on hers.

"I've got you," he said.

"You came for us," she choked out as he pulled her into his arms.

Vaguely she was aware of a chopper hovering overhead. A spotlight sweeping down. Cold wind and spray lashed them. But it was the strength and warmth emanating from Madrid's body into hers that she felt all the way to her heart.

"How did you manage?" she asked, referring to the rescue.

Madrid smiled down at her. "I had a little bit of help."

"Vanderpol?"

He nodded. "Looks like the agency came through, too."

The realization of just how close she and Nicolas had come to dying shook her all over again. "My God, they were going to—"

"It's okay," he said. "They didn't."

Shaking the horrible thoughts from her mind, she looked around. "Where's Nicolas?"

Madrid motioned to where Chin Lee and the boy huddled beneath a blanket. "He's going to be okay."

Jess blinked back tears. "You saved our lives," she whispered.

"I had my own selfish reasons."

She choked out a laugh. "I'm glad."

He pulled her closer. "I'm never going to let you go. Think you can live with that?"

"I can't live without it." She smiled. "I can't live without you."

"Can I get that in writing?"

"I have a better idea," she said, and pulled his mouth down to hers.

Epilogue

One month later

The small chapel was packed. Madrid paced the marble hall outside the rectory and tried hard not to be nervous. He found it ironic that he'd faced down some of the most dangerous criminals the underworld could produce. But here he was about to marry the woman he loved and he'd suddenly been attacked by a bad case of nerves.

"Well, you're a hell of a sight to behold."

He looked up at the sound of Sean Cutter's voice. His superior wore a black tuxedo and looked every bit as uncomfortable as Madrid felt.

"I'm glad you could make it," he said.

"Wouldn't miss it for the world." The two men shook hands, their gazes locking. "She's gorgeous."

Madrid shoved his hands into his pockets. "I don't know what the hell she wants with me."

Cutter grinned. "I guess that's one of those mysteries we'll probably never figure out." Removing an envelope from the inside pocket of his tux, he passed it to Madrid.

"What's this?" he asked.

"Open it and find out."

Madrid tore open the envelope, pulled out the single sheet of paper printed on official MIDNIGHT Agency letterhead and quickly read. He wasn't an emotional man, but for a moment he couldn't speak. "You're promoting me?"

"You earned it." Cutter grimaced. "You followed your instincts on the Lighthouse Point PD case. You did the right thing against tremendous odds." He sighed. "Against pressure from your superiors." He looked down, then met Madrid's gaze. "I was wrong."

Madrid didn't know what to say. A month ago when he'd laid down his badge and gun, he'd thought his career with the MIDNIGHT Agency was over. "Thanks," he managed.

"Norm Mummert and most of the officers working for him are behind bars as of last week. The corruption had penetrated all levels of the Lighthouse Point PD and another small police department with partial jurisdiction over Humboldt Bay. It was one of the most far-reaching cases of police corruption the agency has ever seen. Prosecutors say it's going to be a slam dunk."

"What about Capricorn and Yates?"

"Jake Vanderpol took Yates into custody yesterday in Paris. So far as we can tell, Capricorn in clean."

"What about the women?" he asked, referring to the young immigrants who had been smuggled into the United States using Capricorn container ships in Luna Bay, Lighthouse Point and Humboldt Bay to the north.

"Most of them have been reunited with their families."

Madrid was overwhelmed by a powerful sense of gratification knowing justice had prevailed. "I couldn't have done it without Jess and Nicolas."

"Jess received a formal apology from the governor of California for what local law enforcement put her and the boy through."

"I'm glad."

Through the closed doors leading into the nave where dozens of people had gathered for the celebration, they heard the organ begin the traditional wedding march.

Cutter cleared his throat. "You've got the next three weeks off," he said. "I suggest you use them wisely, because I'm going to work your butt off once you're back."

Madrid couldn't help it; he smiled. He thought of Jess waiting for him beyond those doors. He thought of little Nicolas, and for the second time in two minutes he found himself fighting emotion.

"After the wedding today, the three of us are flying to Hawaii for some R and R," he said.

"You're adopting the boy?"

Madrid nodded. "We're crazy about him. He's a great kid."

"Angela would have been pleased." Cutter crossed to the ornately carved doors. "Ready?"

"I've been ready my whole life."

Cutter swung open the doors. "Good luck, man."

Entering the nave, Mike Madrid stepped into his future, his destiny, his fate. And in that moment he was the happiest man in the world.

* * * * *

*Set in darkness beyond the ordinary world.
Passionate tales of life and death.
With characters' lives ruled by laws the everyday
world can't begin to imagine.*

Introducing NOCTURNE, *a spine-tingling new line
from Silhouette Books.*

The thrills and chills begin with
UNFORGIVEN
by Lindsay McKenna

Plucked from the depths of hell, former military sharp-shooter Reno Manchahi was hired by the government to kill a thief, but he had a mission of his own. Descended from a family of shape-shifters, Reno vowed to get the revenge he'd thirsted for all these years. But his mission went awry when his target turned out to be a powerful seductress, Magdalena Calen Hernandez, who risked everything to battle a potent evil. Suddenly, Reno had to transform himself into a true hero and fight the enemy that threatened them all. He had to become a Warrior for the Light....

*Turn the page for a sneak preview of
UNFORGIVEN by Lindsay McKenna.
On sale September 26,
wherever books are sold.*

Chapter 1

One shot...one kill.

The sixteen-pound sledgehammer came down with such fierce power that the granite boulder shattered instantly. A spray of glittering mica exploded into the air and sparkled momentarily around the man who wielded the tool as if it were a weapon. Sweat ran in rivulets down Reno Manchahi's drawn, intense face. Naked from the waist up, the hot July sun beating down on his back, he hefted the sledgehammer skyward once more. Muscles in his thick forearms leaped and biceps bulged. Even his breath was focused on the boulder. In his mind's eye, he pictured Army General Robert Hampton's fleshy, arrogant fifty-year-old features on the rock's surface. Air exploded from between his lips as he brought the avenging hammer down. The boulder pulverized beneath his funneled hatred.

One shot...one kill...

Nostrils flaring, he inhaled the dank, humid heat and drew it deep into his massive lungs. Revenge allowed Reno to endure his imprisonment at a U.S. Navy brig near San Diego, California. Drops of sweat were flung in all directions as the crack of his sledgehammer claimed a third stone victim. Mouth taut, Reno moved to the next boulder.

The other prisoners in the stone yard gave him a wide berth. They always did. They instinctively felt his simmering hatred, the palpable revenge in his cinnamon-colored eyes, was more than skin-deep.

And they whispered he was different.

Reno enjoyed being a loner for good reason. He came from a medicine family of shape-shifters. But even this secret power had not protected him—or his family. His wife, Ilona, and his three-year-old daughter, Sarah, were dead. Murdered by Army General Hampton in their former home on USMC base in Camp Pendleton, California. Bitterness thrummed through Reno as he savagely pushed the toe of his scarred leather boot against several smaller pieces of gray granite that were in his way.

The sun beat down upon Manchahi's naked

shoulders, grown dark red over time, shouting his half-Apache heritage. With his straight black hair grazing his thick shoulders, copper skin and broad face with high cheekbones, everyone knew he was Indian. When he'd first arrived at the brig, some of the prisoners taunted him and called him Geronimo. Something strange happened to Reno during his fight with the name-calling prisoners. Leaning down after he'd won the scuffle, he'd snarled into each of their bloodied faces that if they were going to call him anything, they would call him *gan,* which was the Apache word for *devil*.

His attackers had been shocked by the wounds on their faces, the deep claw marks. Reno recalled doubling his fist as they'd attacked him en masse. In that split second, he'd gone into an altered state of consciousness. In times of danger, he transformed into a jaguar. A deep, growling sound had emitted from his throat as he defended himself in the three-against-one fracas. It all happened so fast that he thought he had imagined it. He'd seen his hands morph into a forearm and paw, claws extended. The slashes left on the three men's faces after the fight told him he'd begun to shape-shift. A fist made bruises and swelling;

not four perfect, deep claw marks. Stunned and anxious, he hid the knowledge of what else he was from these prisoners. Reno's only defense was to make all the prisoners so damned scared of him and remain a loner.

Alone. Yeah, he was alone, all right. The steel hammer swept downward with hellish ferocity. As the granite groaned in protest, Reno shut his eyes for just a moment. Sweat dripped off his nose and square chin.

Straightening, he wiped his furrowed, wet brow and looked into the pale blue sky. What got his attention was the startling cry of a red-tailed hawk as it flew over the brig yard. Squinting, he watched the bird. Reno could make out the rust-colored tail on the hawk. As a kid growing up on the Apache reservation in Arizona, Reno knew that all animals that appeared before him were messengers.

Brother, what message do you bring me? Reno knew one had to ask in order to receive. Allowing the sledgehammer to drop to his side, he concentrated on the hawk who wheeled in tightening circles above him.

Freedom! the hawk cried in return.

Reno shook his head, his black hair moving against his broad, thickset shoulders. *Freedom?*

No way, Brother. No way. Figuring that he was making up the hawk's shrill message, Reno turned away. Back to his rocks. Back to picturing Hampton's smug face.

Freedom!

Look for UNFORGIVEN
by Lindsay McKenna,
the spine-tingling launch title
from Silhouette Nocturne™.
Available September 26,
wherever books are sold.

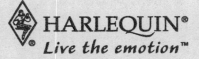

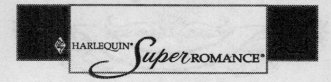

Harlequin Historicals®
Historical Romantic Adventure!

From rugged lawmen and valiant knights to defiant heiresses and spirited frontierswomen, Harlequin Historicals will capture your imagination with their dramatic scope, passion and adventure.

Harlequin Historicals... they're too good to miss!

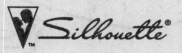